Washing Dishes in Hotel Paradise

Washing Dishes
in Hotel Paradise

Eduardo Belgrano Rawson

Translated by Rosie Marteau

Hesperus Worldwide

Hesperus Worldwide
Published by Hesperus Press Limited
4 Rickett Street, London sw6 1ru
www.hesperuspress.com

Washing Dishes in Hotel Paradise first published in Spanish
as *El mundo se derrumba y nosotros nos enamoramos* in 2006

This translation first published by Hesperus Press Limited, 2010

El mundo se derrumba y nosotros nos enamoramos
© Eduardo Belgrano Rawson, 2006

This translation published by arrangement with Literatische Agentur Mertin
Inh. Nicole e. K., Frankfurt am Main, Germany

English language translation © Rosie Marteau, 2010

Work published within the framework of 'Sur' Translation Support Program
of the Ministry of Foreign Affairs, International Trade and Worship of the
Argentine Republic

Designed and typeset by Fraser Muggeridge studio
Printed in Jordan by Jordan National Press

ISBN: 978-1-84391-853-0

Contents

Washing Dishes
in Hotel Paradise

It Wasn't Pacheco

Where did I get all this rubbish from, my grandma asked me one day. She had filled me with stories, but I'd taken no notice. Maybe, thinking about it, because they were too neat. You really need an idea that unravels as it goes along. Didn't the late Chandler say that a story has to be distilled?

Other people's conversations don't contribute much either. People always say the same things. You can't even get anything good out of a tapped phoneline. Some conversations seem carbon copied, like the ones that keep those broken marriages going, when couples meet to share twisted arguments in some cake shop or other in the centre of town.

What you've got left are those seedy rumours overheard on the bus, like the one about the rats on trays that had been spotted lately in the freezers of Chinese restaurants. Or that famous wedding that ended in scandal; I don't know if you remember. When the priest asked that well-worn question (to speak now or forever hold your peace) a guy in the back row jumped up like a scorpion, supposing that a scorpion does actually jump like that. After calling the bride a whore, he screamed at her about everything and anything. Then the family stepped in and there was a pitched battle in the atrium.

Sometimes these rumours can acquire such virulence that they end up appearing in the newspaper. Sometimes the same newspaper takes it upon itself to quash them. This happened with the wedding in question. After reporting the scandal, the press did an about turn. 'There was no such wedding,' the paper had to admit. I think it was *La Nación*. The very same columnist reflected, 'Since when do they ask if anyone has anything to say at a wedding?'

The juicier the gossip, the quicker it gets crushed. Or occasionally it will have a resurgence. 'Did you know that the sewers of

Buenos Aires are full of iguanas?' I heard a girl say. So they tell me. This is a recycled rumour that used to be peddled around New York about thirty years ago. There too it came about because people were getting rid of their pets. Only it was alligators, not iguanas. Somebody flushed some babies down the loo with said results. There was even a movie about it. I could carry on, but there'd be no point. All of those tall tales get forgotten in a sigh. The really good ones never turn into gossip; they tend to die out with their protagonists.

I heard something once that I'd rather not have heard. It had conflict and a punch-line like all those stories my grandma used to tell me. It could be summarised in three lines, like all the best dramas. It might take me a few more. Better I don't say when it happened. I can only reveal that it came from across the ocean. It took place on board a boat: a typical sea-borne drama, if you will. I'd have to be Joseph Conrad to tell it as it should be told, but we'll make do.

We were leaving via the Río de la Plata in that sailboat that smelt of old, wet swine. My companion smelt just the same. Much like my grandma, who used to leave a sprig of pennyroyal and mint amongst clean sheets, he always kept a ship's sail in the depths of the hold. Consequently his shirts stank like an old steamboat.

'I'll steer,' he said. 'You write in peace.'

We were travelling along the Uruguayan coast. My companion thought that during this short voyage one could finally start his Maritime Novel. But one was seasick. Suddenly the radio cut in:

'Pacheco LPQ, Pacheco LPQ,' or something like that. Somebody, perhaps a merchant sailor, wanted to call home. Over the next hour we would be sent crazy by his calls to the link channel, a coastal station known as Pacheco. If you wanted to communicate from the ocean, you had to go via Pacheco.

4

Our own radio equipment was the only fancy bit of the old banger. Thirty years earlier it had been the best boat on the river; now it had fallen on hard times. It was all my companion had left after having lost his job, his third wife and an apartment in Palermo. So that sunny September we were leaving the coast of San Isidro behind us. A tragedy at sea was approaching, but we carried on in the best of all possible worlds.

It was a Tuesday morning. Sailing midweek is delightful. I know thousands of stories about the 'floaters', river wanderers who, like myself, set sail on a working day. One guy had a girlfriend in Colonia on the other side of the river. Every Friday he would set out in his little boat to visit her. He would buy a bag of peanuts at the port and knit a jumper to kill time during the crossing. There are all sorts on the river.

And then there was a small number of yachts with radios. You had to be either a tycoon or bankrupt like my companion to have something like that. The river was a convivial place. Today the ether is teeming with people ranting and raving to anyone who will listen. There is even a lady simulating charming orgasms. Other radios are shouting back at her. You couldn't fit another word on the emergency channel: it was a good job that nobody needed any help. If the Titanic were to sink again one day it would go unnoticed here.

'Pacheco LPQ,' said the voice.

When Pacheco's operator answered the ship's call, he instructed him to switch to Channel 25. We did so too, allowing us to listen in on that foreign conversation that came from beyond the seas. It occurred to me how wonderful it was to be able to call one's own home from the Indian Ocean, even if it did mean airing things in public.

'I'll put you through,' said Pacheco. Once the connection had been made you could almost hear each man breathing. We listened to the telephone ringing until the receiver was picked up and a man's voice said:

'Hello?'

There was a horrified silence. The voice from the boat sounded puzzled.

'Who is this?' he asked.

Another hell of a silence. And then, clearly, we heard the house phone being put down.

'They hung up, sir,' said the operator of Radio Pacheco, suddenly pleasant.

'What do you mean they hung up? Did you ring the number I gave you?'

'Yes sir, I rang that number,' the operator said, coolly, perhaps even with a touch of satisfaction. He then recited each of the six numbers one by one.

'You must have made a mistake...' said the voice from the boat.

'No, sir,' said Pacheco.

'Try again, would you?'

There was such a gentle northerly wind that the water was barely lapping. My companion steered noiselessly, his eyes fixed on the sails. The operator of Pacheco had become a whirlwind of efficiency. He dialled again so quickly that there was no time to think. The telephone rang five times.

'Hello?' said a woman's voice.

'Hello,' replied the voice from the boat.

We daren't even breathe.

'Darling... How are you?'

'Who just answered?' said the voice from the boat.

'What do you mean who just answered?'

'A man answered.'

'No!' she said. 'There must have been a mistake.'

'The phone sounded like the house phone.'

'Are you crazy?'

'A man picked up and said hello...'

'I swear to you...'

'Please...'

'Oh, my love!'

'I'd rather you hung up than treated me like an idiot.'

'The phone didn't even ring!...' she pleaded.

Her voice sounded desperate. It made him want to hold her.

'It must have been Pacheco,' he murmured.

And then, like a cobra ready to attack, the operator of Pacheco came back onto the line:

'It – was – n't – Pa – che – co,' he declared.

Every time I recall this dialogue a chill runs down my spine. It's been a long time, but their voices are still with me (*it wasn't Pacheco*). I imagine her in the bedroom, lying completely naked on the bed, repentant and beautiful, in love in spite of everything, her eyes pricked with tears. I see the gentleman on the boat gently pass the microphone back to the vespertine operator and return outside with all the dignity of a man, taking his place on deck under the starlit night. I can see the other idiot between the sheets, letting his last cigarette burn out, cursing himself under his breath.

Other times I tell myself that it wasn't like that. That there was no such man in the bed. That nobody hung up the phone. That it was all a dirty trick on the part of the operator of Pacheco.

But I can't even convince myself.

The Countess of Chernobyl

I frequent a rough bar, which every so often ends up with a bus ploughing into it. Once, so the barmen say, a cashier who had been sacked returned with a fire axe and buried it in the skull of a lady who was about to stifle a tear. But he was out of it, and that was another story.

The worst thing about the bar is the toilets. You get there surrounded by subterranean sounds via a narrow passageway that opens out into a cavern crammed with clients peering sideways. You piss urgently. One day when you least expect it, you figure, there'll be a raid down there. These toilets must be a punishment intended for men of little fortune. As to very young writers, I'd suggest they never set foot in there unless accompanied by their mothers.

When I get back from the bathroom a slim, languid woman is sitting at the next table, chain smoking cigarettes. She has a packet of Gitanes in front of her. I'm dying to say something to her, but I don't even try. I stay hung on her every glance, until she pays and leaves. I spend half the morning unable to finish a single line.

Every now and again I watch from my table as some local lies in wait, readying himself to cross the road. These urban trackers have incredible instincts. They can tell from four streets away if the one that they can see up ahead is a 60 or a 38. They can leap from a moving underground train without taking their eyes off the newspaper. They trot alongside the bus with a copy of the *Crónica* under their arm and jump on at exactly the right moment with the elegance of an Indian. They never fall. They know every corner of the jungle better than their own hands. They know just when they can cross death row's corridor without being crushed by the stampede.

They are the Cheyennes of Buenos Aires. The city is bankrupt. The former gold prospectors have become tin gatherers. I always wanted to write about these creatures, but thanks to a lack of imagination, I turned to science fiction. Right now I'm concocting something that takes place twenty years in the future. Buenos Aires is surrounded by an electric fence like the Mexican border. Fires burn on the horizon. They are the immigrant settlements: New Berlin, New Washington, New London. Every night the immigrants attempt to steal through and are stopped by gunfire. It's an action story, and the best places to write these are downtown dives.

Writers' haunts aren't good enough. You freeze in winter and suffocate in summer. From midday the café is burning up. There are some advantages: in El Tortoni you can order cider on tap and *leche merengada* with cinnamon, plus it's one of the few bars in the world that serves *maté* infusions.

My bar is in Tribunales. It's a typical den of iniquity. The barman calls his customers 'doctor'. Some people go there exclusively to be 'doctored' by the barman. It's a hideout for starving lawyers, so much so that there is a Remington shaver behind the bar. From time to time someone drops in to type his desperate manuscript. The customer hangs back with the look of a prisoner on remand. Now the typewriter falls silent. In the window seat, a lawyer and his accomplice talk business. 'He asked to have a look at the case notes and then, when the clerks' backs were turned, he swallowed the contracts!' summarised the more senior of the pair. And there the story ends. The other one swills his coffee around in the cup. Something is eating him up.

'Goyena called me again last night,' he murmurs at last. 'There was a copper at the door, ringing the bell. She wanted to know what to do. Can you believe it? Four o'clock in the morning, and it even woke the twins up... my wife asked who it was. "Wait one moment while I have a look at my Statutes book," I said out loud. But what could I really tell her? I got out of there sharpish.'

The skinny Gitanes girl is called Samantha. We soon make friends. She works as a living statue in Palermo Hollywood, but lives nearby. She was in England before. She'd learned her trade in Covent Garden. The competition there is terrible. While Samantha would draw in a couple of little old ladies and a boy, the smoking fire-eater never had fewer than forty spectators. That's why she ended up coming back. Here statues are worth nothing: at first she was knocked over by two kids on skates. Later a dog started to come and pee on her at the same time every day, a dog with an owner and everything, who didn't even lift a finger to stop him. Now she has a Ukrainian boyfriend who plays the violin in the underground. Like all the Russian buskers swarming about lately, he'd been first violinist in the Leningrad Symphony Orchestra. We chatted across tables while Samantha waited for him to arrive.

When I say bars, I mean those in Buenos Aires. The little cafés inland are different. In Cordoba for example, some years back, if you went around with a notebook and pen you had to be a dodgy bookie. But there was a special place, half café, half pizzeria, that we shared with the author of the Great Cordoban Novel. His work had already taken ten years, and it was going to have it all, from the Spanish settlers to the storytellers who still fought to amuse despite the presiding poverty. But he died before he could finish it.

Out of all the well-known bars, it was the last place you'd start telling stories. It already had its own conflict. Sometimes it would burst with drama, something that couldn't be said for our own colourless narratives. Once, in full view of everyone, the following took place:

I was at the bar, wrestling with the fourth chapter. At the other end of the bar the author of the GNC[1] scratched his head.

Huddled by the door, two friends of mine who lived over the road were killing their hunger with coffee. A guy who had just come in walked up to the bar. He was carrying something that he showed to the landlord. It was a bag from King of Chicken. 'Can you watch this for me for a bit?' he asked. It turned out he was going to the cinema and didn't want to take it with him. The landlord took the bag. Let's say he was called Ismael. Ismael put the bag in the fridge. As the guy left, I noticed my friends' faces gleaming. It was obvious they were watching intently. The fragrance of roast chicken had set them alight. I went back to my work. When I surfaced again, my friends had left.

In a while another guy came in, a friend of the friends, a volunteer for such suicide missions. He was also a friend of mine. He stole past me like lightning – he didn't even catch my eye. He stood opposite Ismael and said, 'I've come on behalf of the man with the chicken. I think he's had some problem at home. He asked if you would hand it over to me.' Ismael turned and bent down with pure apathy, reached into the fridge and handed over the bag of chicken.

But I was already far from there, swept away by the odyssey of a man who calls home from the high seas. You know how it is when a story works. Time splits open. You read the page again and when you finally lift your head three hours have gone by. By the time I realised what had happened, my friends had come back, sat back at the same old table. They had demolished the chicken. They'd only had to add three portions of chips and a bottle of wine. They settled in serenely to wait for the exodus from the cinema.

When the chicken guy came back, Ismael was in his usual pose, staring into his black future. He gave absolutely no signal for anyone to come between him and his nightmare. For a couple of minutes the outsider stood in front of the bar, waiting patiently.

Ismael didn't bat an eyelid. The outsider appealed to the last smile he had left within him: 'I'm the man with the chicken, don't you remember me?'

I'm not up to describing the unprecedented ferociousness of what happened next. There are no words to express Ismael's pallor as he gripped the bar towel, or how his eyes took on the opaque tone of an amoral shark's. Suddenly the man from the cinema, cutting the heated discussion short, unleashed this terrible phrase: 'You son of a bitch. You want to keep the chicken.'

You have to talk about the war without mentioning it, don't you? And then there's that whole iceberg thing. It's what goes unsaid that matters. And you can't go around killing people just for the sake of it. Better one dead than ten. And as to killing, it's got to be done well. Because to make matters worse, you always slip up in action scenes. For all these reasons, so difficult to articulate, for the moment I won't say another word.

When I leave the bar that I hang out in, I don't feel sad. Nor do I feel empty, like Hemingway after making love. I feel fortunate instead, and keen to forge ahead. Only that then comes the worst bit: dumping everything I've written into the computer.

There's this kid who usually lends me a hand when the machine packs up. He's just turned thirteen, he's read every book that exists and he's planning to retire the most famous writer of all time. As he demonstrates, he only needs a few seconds to identify every instance that you used the same word in a book. And that's not all: he's just done it for Borges. 'First you scan the text,' he explains as he copies *El Aleph*. 'Afterwards you paste it here. Then you click *search*.' And it starts doing it just like that, while he taps his fingers. The repetitions are highlighted on the screen. 'What a bastard…' he mutters, at the height of the excitement.

These sorts of people scare me. That's why I keep editing – the first versions are always horrendous. It's probably because I write them in bars and Buenos Aires never lets you come up for air.

I might leave all this behind one day. I know this place in the mountains. There are walnut trees from various centuries and streams with little waterfalls. Partridges everywhere. From time to time a fox passes by with a pear in its mouth. I might move there to write something, and it won't have typhoons or anything and it will be about the blue mountains and the tractors perspiring at dusk and January falcons nesting in the forests.

But I always end up going back to my cave in Tribunales. Samantha's still at her table. We keep each other company until the Ukrainian arrives. But he never does. There's no boyfriend any more, she declares. He left her for a sword-swallower. It seems a shame, because they were making a killing on the train line to Tigre.

Samantha would play the atomic ruin. The Ukrainian would carry her in his arms along the carriages, lay her on the ground and explain her tragedy, then follow it by playing an adagio by Khatchaturian. She didn't even move a single hair. People couldn't take their eyes off of her. She played her part after all. Stretched out there on the ground, in leather boots and a bonnet, she must have seemed like the Countess of Siberia, paralysed by atomic emissions. The only movement that you could see on her entire body was a tear that rolled from her eye at the end of the adagio. 'A single tear,' clarified Samantha, who could even control her bodily fluids.

With that she paid her tab and left. I grab my pencil and write: *The Countess of Chernobyl*.

Way of a Gaucho

I just watched it on telly. It's a typical Hollywood concoction about the tribulations of a gaucho. With Gene Tierney and Rory Calhoun. It's got all the usual forts and Indians, but it lacks at least a dog. Filming in the Pampas without a dog somewhere in the cast must be like filming *2001* without the moon making an appearance, but that's why special effects were invented. And after all, it is by the same director as *The Mark of the Panther*.

What else can you say about *Way of a Gaucho*? Nothing, except that Gene was as beautiful as the time that she turned up in the flesh in a café in my town. She was sipping a *racauchi* cola² in the company of Rory and the gaucho Amieva, nestled in the window. I can still see them at that table, even after all this time. Rory was a second-rate actor, a counterfeit Robert Taylor, who was the best in those days. And as for Gene… Well, she was the fourth goddess of cinema, although her star was in decline. Ali Khan had already left her, but at least she wasn't so confused. Now, having discovered her on the telly, something had been set free inside of me. It turns out that *Way of a Gaucho*, along with some other piece of tosh 'made in Argentina' that also came out around then, had, in a way, led me to take up this line of work.

I write for want of anything better to do. Plus, I'm one of those people who can't get movies out of their heads. It must be because one can never put exactly the right music to the text. And without the music, as you know, you've only got half a film. I first began to dream in cinemascope on my graduate fieldtrip when we saw *Taras Bulba* at some pass in the North. With Yul Brinner, Christine Kaufmann and Tony Curtis. A friend from Salta had taken us to the shoot, because she was renting her house out to the director. We arrived on set just before midday.

Things were going badly. Something was up. The technical team looked desperate. They were going for the tenth take. Tony lay crushed on the ground, with Christine weeping over him. (How sexy was that blonde?) Profound silence all around; it was being recorded live. People spoke in whispers. Tony's eyes were watering because of the sun's glare. He must already have been thinking about leaving his wife to run off with the German girl. Christine was about eighteen. (She effectively kept Tony for herself. This hurt Janet Leigh more than the stab wounds that Norman Bates would later deliver her in *Psycho*. Right in the middle of filming *Taras*, Janet went back to the US with her heart in pieces.)

When everything was ready, the spotlights lit up. The director went like *that* with his eyelids, which meant action. The camera was already rolling. Then a dark-skinned Indian from Salta, buried in the crowds like Atahualpa's Incas lying in wait to ambush the Spanish, shrouded in his coca farmer's hood, began to curse imperialism with the most disgusting expletives ever uttered in the Calchaquíes Valleys, focusing above all on the director's mother.

'Cut! Cut!...' cried the director, who was no other than J. Lee Thompson (*The Guns of Navarone*).

The Indian had been hanging around the hills for weeks without letting them shoot anything. As soon as the camera got going, he started swearing. They'd tried everything, even filming with their backs to the actors and a blanket covering the camera, but it was impossible to trick him, so much so that the director decided to move on to something else. A Mexican came out with a megaphone and called the extras. There were about two thousand of them, a mixture of gauchos and Incas disguised as Cossacks, all social outcasts, who would soon get up and carry on fighting even though they'd already been killed.

'Gauchos,' pleaded the guy with the megaphone, swearing in his Mexican dialect. 'We're going to do the battle scene right now, so please come over here.'

The Indian didn't matter to him at all any more, nor his insults, which he figured may even have helped him out with the battle cries when they were mixed in to the sound track. That's what happens to desperate people, driven to make the best of misfortune.

'Gentlemen, gauchos, it's already getting late,' he insisted. 'Can you all get together?'

The gauchos took no notice. The Mexican wasn't sweating blood yet, but he could already envisage himself back in Tijuana, dishing out quesadillas. The producers chose the place because the extras were cheap. Ignorance was bliss. Atahualpa's gaucho rabble were still scattered about, knelt on their haunches chatting or dozing by the cacti with their horses to hand. The dozers were so crestfallen and bereft that they seemed about to plant a kiss on the earth. They were the extras with their horses. They were the warriors of *Taras Bulba*. It was a typical Saltan November, hot and dry.

As the day was a write-off, Yul got back into his trailer and we didn't see head nor tail of him for the rest of the day. Tony vanished too. His second double, a country boy with bright eyes, was left to rule the roost. With no Tony around, the girls from my school settled for the Saltan. He was better than Tony, according to the make-up artist. Everybody said that he had gone down on the producer's daughter. Tony had three doubles. He was one of those inept types that even demanded a double just to touch his horse. The sun set slowly behind Taras castle, which cost millions of dollars despite being made of cardboard. The gauchos remained strewn about until we left the site.

So ended our encounter with *Taras Bulba*. At night, in the hotel, our heads were spinning with gauchos as Cossacks and foul-mouthed Andean Indians. The servant in particular seemed pretty inspired. It was the first night of our school trip in Salta.

What are you supposed to make of a hotchpotch like that? To top it all, everything was mixed up with another ghost from my past that wouldn't let me rest.

I mean *Way of a Gaucho*. The film with Gene Tierney. Who, as I said, appeared to me one day in a café in town. I should make it clear that this was long before *Taras*, when everything was much rosier. To start with, I was nine years old. I was being pulled along by my dad one gloriously sunny Sunday soon after mass, on the way to have a *racauchi*. I can still imagine my face, with that happiness that comes from walking along with your dad. We were nearly at the *Sportsman* when the vision stopped us dead. The goddess was at the window-table, along with two others. The gangsters had gone downtown. My dad put the brakes on. 'That's Gene,' he announced, while I stood drooling on the pavement. Suddenly they spotted us. She offered the most tender and melancholy smile that you could possibly give to an idiot. A cold front swept through my calves. I fell so in love that I could never recover. For years I saw myself on top of Gene whispering, 'Ay luv yú,' while she, with her eyes rolled back, moaned, 'Ay luv yú tú.' But on the day of our encounter, I wasn't ready for all that yet. Spring was coming to an end. Gene was with Rory Calhoun and the gaucho Amieva, drinking her *racauchi* with ice instead of a real coke, because witchcraft was banned then in La Punta, along with boxing and homeopathy, and all, we used to say, because Coca Cola wouldn't reveal the formula. So there we were, ripped off but proud, with our *racauchi*. Nobody knew what it was and it didn't even have a formula.

The *Sportsman* thing was that Sunday. I never saw Gene Tierney again, and I didn't hear anything about the movie coming out either. They disappeared from the town just as they had arrived.

So, on returning to Salta after *Taras*, my legs weren't long enough to follow the tracks left by *Way of a Gaucho*. I wanted to find out everything I could about that mysterious shoot. But no one in La Punta mentioned it any more. Ten years had gone by, which back then equated to half a lifetime. I couldn't even track down gaucho Amieva who'd been tarting about dressed as a cowboy since he fell in love with a girl: Stetson, boots and breeches. He was head honcho of the area where they shot the movie. Who knew how I could find him. I was hounded by a nightmare. I couldn't stop imagining the gaucho giving it to her in the corral.

I forged ahead regardless. Kiko Luna lent me a hand. One day we got a tip-off. El Negro de la Susana, illiterate by parentage, had worked as an extra on *Way of a Gaucho*, so we ran off to see him in the Carcocha district. It turned out to be an inopportune moment. El Negro, in a vest and underpants, lay dead in the bed, as if lost in the music of his Franklin radio's valves. He barely even glanced at us. His answers were vague. *Way of a Gaucho? No, mate. Nothing to do with me.* The closest he'd got to cinema was the time he'd driven the *racauchi* truck to the film set. They chucked some little role his way, but he'd refused it. After making his point he settled back into bed face down and may have fallen asleep, so we hit the road.

We went back home. Kiko was intrigued. 'May I ask what the fuck you're looking for?' he asked me. 'Nothing. I'm a novelist,' I said. 'What?' 'I'm going to write a book,' I explained. After mulling it over for a moment, Kiko, who hated being quiet, took the lead again: 'I've got a better story.' He was a crap storyteller. Then he asked me, in cold blood, 'Do you remember Lucila's wedding?' 'Which Lucila?' I asked, as if I didn't know. 'My sister,' said Kiko. 'The one at the house?' I suggested. (My house, which you reached by one street and left by another, was the venue for family weddings.) 'Exactly,' nodded Kiko, who might as well have been a cousin. 'The shit-fest?' I added to clear up any confusion. 'The very same.' This said, Kiko swallowed and declared, 'It was me that spiked the mulled wine with horse laxative.'

Bloody bastard. I quickly forgot all about Gene Tierney. An age-old enigma was suddenly laid bare. To think we'd spent night after night trying to work out who was behind that particular exploit. Now here he was in front of me. Kiko didn't spare me the detail. He described his every move throughout the course of the party, from the moment he threw the laxative into the pot to locking the bathroom doors and flinging the keys up onto the roof. The guests included everyone from the Governor to the Bishop. Every last corner of the garden was mercilessly illuminated. To make matters worse it was a sweltering night, so it wasn't long before the mulled wine was flowing. The pavement was packed with onlookers, who peered through the iron gates. Put simply, the whole thing happened in full view of the mob, amidst applause, among groans and curses, from high above the treetops and all along the flowerbeds. The Bishop hadn't even managed four steps when the eruption began. The bride, in particular, shat all over the begonias. Kiko turned a marriage into absolutely magical chaos.

There was my novel. I could hardly wait to go home and get started. Only now everything had changed. It wouldn't be a production in cinemascope with Gene Tierney and Tony Curtis, but a story with aunties and cousins, the kind that swamp weddings. That's the tragedy of stories, that they always do their own thing and end up where you least expect it.

'What are you going to call it?' asked everyone at home, because it was back when nothing went unannounced. I kept it quiet just in case, as I had a feeling that the stupidest ideas are always the first to strike. But that night, I had it:

Don't Disturb Your Heart.
With Adrián Mondragón, Isabel Harnero and Evaristo Pedregosa.

But *something* told me that I was missing something, that there were more strands to the story, which may well pass through the Carcocha quarter, along with El Negro de la Susana's leap to stardom and the heat between the gaucho and Gene. These sorts of doubts always gnaw at novice writers who want to tell it all. And what's worse, El Negro was hiding a secret. He was lying when he said he'd rejected the role. In fact, he'd been in front of the camera for three hours. I had recently found this out; Susana herself, who turned out to be his mother, told me. He'd been a step away from becoming Fox's new leading man. El Negro had the best gaucho face in the whole history of Hollywood.

This is what happened. It seems they had him stand on the road, with the cameras rolling. It was a silent take. The Negro just had to stare into the distance. For a few moments everything went perfectly, until the Negro started pissing about with his hand.

They wanted to cut his nuts off. Ten times they told him to keep still and every time he proceeded to do the same thing. 'Cut! Cut! Cut, for crying out loud!' the director shouted. 'Who told you to do that?' they all spat. The idiot just kept raising his hand, as if he was leaving forever. 'Listen, are you stupid or what?' someone else said. 'What if we tie it to his belt?' the cameramen suggested. It wasn't as if he was waving it about: he just lifted it. 'Where did they pull this Indian from?' an electrician chimed in. 'Oh My God,' sighed a queer from the make-up department. Everyone else shouted in chorus. The Negro stood on the road, finding their blindness incomprehensible. This, as he saw it, was your stock farewell, but his protest fell on deaf ears. Fox had its own guidelines for conveying human emotions. If you want to express anything, an assistant explained to the Negro, you do it with your eyes. But nobody thought to pass on these wise words in Spanish. So it was that soon afterwards the gaucho's cattle gates opened to let the soda truck pass through with the Negro de la Susana at the wheel, focused grimly on the road ahead as he moved towards an uncertain twilight, his ranger's hat covering his eyes, soft music in the background, maybe something by Mantovani, in what might as well have been a kiss goodbye to the Oscar.

Only Love Can Save You

I have a friend who has checked himself in to a spa in the mountains again. For the first time in his life he seems determined to complete the treatment. It's his fourth relapse. He's depressed, they say. He's spent the night in his wife's arms, who visits him regularly. His eyes are wide and dark. It's not that he feels in danger or anything. He might be one of the few that hasn't felt the bullets whizzing past him yet. Up until now, he hasn't been mentioned in the papers. But he has come to accept that he has a terrible addiction. 'I'm telling you, he can't stop,' his wife sobs on the phone. That's why he's in the spa in the mountains, the only one that offers a serious plan for giving up robbery.

It was the same old story. We've been friends since he was four years old, when he swallowed his dad's pay cheque along with a bee and a match. They blamed thieves, but the truth soon came out. No one locked their doors around there in those days. In fact, his house didn't even have a front door. There were two gays in the town, someone who took some drug or other, and one girl who'd had an abortion. That was all the sin there was in stock. Us kids went pale just hearing about these things. But now there was a rising star. His name is Danilo. His surname is by the by. Only his best friends spotted the latent drama: making him the Deputy Home Secretary was like letting your starving granny loose at a Buenos Aires 'All You Can Eat' buffet.

At the spa they were given supplements and made to go for an early morning run to get their endorphins going. After a sauna they were given a massage with purifying ointments. The solarium is filled with Andean fragrances, peppermint, pennyroyal and tender *carqueja*.[3] The idea is that the mountain herbs temper their anxieties through exercise and testimony in the Cayman Islands. In group meetings, Danilo has said that if it were up to him, he'd stay there for the rest of his life, watching the mountain goats and the evening tractors. A bit of bread, a glass of wine and a handful of olives. According to his personal trainer that was all the Greeks needed in Plato's time.

His roommate agrees. He is an ex-Director of the Pan-American Anti-Laundering Initiative. He was the Junior Parliament's Young Person of the Year. His trial had just finished. His contacts in the government were worthless (he was the man responsible for carrying the lizard-skin briefcase that later became so famous), so the North Americans decided to hand him over.

The ex-Director's career was meteoric. He started out as a front man. This nearly cost him his head. He had the misfortune of splitting up with the old lady. She demanded half of everything they owned, which of course all belonged to someone else. It was useless trying to explain to her that it was other people's money. These wives don't listen to reason. It took him nearly two years to pay off his wife's spite. The revelations of his roommate made Danilo quake. At least he was lucky enough to count on a wife made of iron who stood shoulder to shoulder with him to fight by his side.

At night the group members play *Fraud!*, a variant of *Monopoly*. The first player to blow a bank wins. In the case of a draw, the victims decide the difference. This is part of the treatment. The Medical Director, himself a great believer in methadone, would run around the rooms handing out the board game.

There are three sorts of patient in the mountain spa: the smokers, the fatties and *them*. But the brain works in the same way, so after the siesta they all get together with the psychologist. The aim is to trawl through childhood. The causes of any turmoil are to be found there. The patients resurface their traumas in whatever way they can, until night falls and the sun sets in the Sierra.

And to top it all, Danilo didn't present with any scars. He had a model childhood. He's still with his wife. I think they've been together since they went to the same playschool. By way of a traumatic experience, or what you'd typically call traumatic, he can't recall anything. The psychologist presses him without success. He later enquires sensitively if there were other addicts in the family.

Danilo doesn't want to let him down, so he makes a real effort to rake up the dirt. It takes quite a lot, given that we're talking about super-healthy families, but he tries anyway. He's not sure if he should mention his Aunt Mítico, who liked a drink. Or his cousin Yeyo, a hardened wanker. He could even get turned on reading *Unesco Post*. His parents were at their wits' end. The case shook the whole family. An aunt based in Brazil sent a little bag of leaves of *adormideira*, very popular in Sao Paolo to ensure that *as crianzas nao se masturben de mais*.[4] (Danilo could still remember his aunt tearing them into little pieces to scatter them all over Yeyo's clothes. The leftover leaves were boiled up. Once his pants had been washed, they had to be hung out to dry without wringing until the sun came up.)

The psychologist listens to the story with noticeable scepticism. For him, if there was a nub to the case, it was the swallowing of the wages. We've all swallowed things, from elastic bands to thermometers. But not one of us has eaten our father's entire wages, overtime and all.

The nutritionist disagrees. She is working on a study. She maintains that Danilo's problem is triggered by a fatty acid deficiency that causes an imbalance in his prostate gland. This was why she included catfish fillets drenched in olive oil in his diet. For his part, the kinesiologist lacks any sort of theory and just gets on with his job. He smears Danilo in mud and goes out to smoke a cigarette. Celeste is waiting for him in the corridor; they're having a romance. He sorts her out with fags and she lets him into her bedroom. The squeals can be heard from outside.

The psychologist reserves a special session for Danilo's group. They all have to confront their first time. Danilo's was in a ministerial bathroom. His memories are hazy. It barely lasted a second. A shadow appeared suddenly in the steamed up window. He was handed something. When he looked up at the mirror again, all he could see was his own reflection. Danilo didn't even return to his office. He went straight home. He remembers walking slowly down the staircase of the Ministry. In his right hand he was carrying a bulky envelope. A4 manila paper: to make things worse, he'd left without his briefcase that morning. His car was waiting for him downstairs. His driver opened the door for him. This scene is replayed in slow motion in his nightmares. Since then he has had panic attacks whenever he sees a staircase or a steamed up mirror.

Danilo will be discharged on Monday. The Director will send them off, as always, with emotive words. He says the same thing to every group: that we succumb to corruption through idleness, so resistance requires a tremendous struggle. Now his graduates will set out armed with new weapons for the struggle: the diet of sighs, the vitamin supplements, the Hungarian massage salts, and the mixture of marine plankton with *jarilla*[5] and donkey's tooth for their immersion baths. All very effective against the syndrome of abstinence. Healthy living and self-imposed restrictions. A positive attitude: this will be the mantra. Strength through adversity. If something goes wrong, they carry a simple saying in their pocket, a personalised prayer, written by the psychologist for times of need.

Maybe it'll work for him. Before they were married, he and his wife prayed frenetically so as not to end up in bed. That was

25

how they'd managed to reach their wedding day as virgins. Danilo is capable of anything for his wife and children. This will save him in the end. The secret is love.

With the Whole World Crumbling, We Pick this Time to Fall in Love

Nacho Alcorta appeared on the bridge, more or less on the line where spies used to do business, right in the heartlands of the old Cold War. These days the bridge swarmed with tourists and lifeguards, where the two Germanys once met. Nacho had a stall on the right side, heading towards East Berlin, where he bought and sold little fragments of The Wall. He also offered items from the Kremlin. This came as no surprise to me; his commercial pursuits in Europe dovetailed perfectly with his most recent engagements in Argentina, namely the illegal exportation of dinosaur eggs and the theft of meteorites that had resided in Patagonia for millions of years. In any case, it was still difficult to spot him, fleecing tourists right in the middle of Oberbambrücke amongst the Turks and Russians from the Volga that descended on Germany in their droves.

Apart from his same old extravagant moustache, this poorly rehashed hippy was just a shadow of my old workmate at the Ateneo Neruda.[6] While I downed my Berliner Weisse sat at a table on the terrace, a group of Belgian tourists readied themselves for the attack. The ladies scrutinised the fake watches with the KGB crest, while the men foraged around among the medals, bayonets and gas masks and the tour guide examined the river below with an antiquated telescope. El Nacho, according to a handwritten sign hanging from his stall, specialised in Red Army surplus paraphernalia. His nearby colleagues kept a close eye on his run of good trade. Now, ready for action, Nacho displayed the same persuasiveness as he did in the old days when we worked in El Ateneo.

Twenty years had gone by, but his jeans looked just like the ones he wore that Cordoban spring, as he shaved in the shade of a stunted pepper plant and I wolfed down a croissant in the barrio's sun. Then we got through the afternoon's schedule together. That day we'd arrived with time to spare before our shift, so Nacho was shaving to pass the time. The scent of orange trees filled the air. The terrace may have been on its last legs, but it sometimes smelt of orange trees or yellow jasmine, which competed with the cat piss that exuded from the crates of empty bottles.

After he'd taken a look at himself in a mirror left on a crate of soft drinks, he made one final stroke over his jaw line and wiped the knife clean with a page of *The Lives of the Saints of Seville* (Niños Expósitos Press, seventeen hundred and something, if memory serves), of which barely a third was left. He ripped the page out carefully, screwed it up into a little ball and tossed it into the black dustbin where the morning staff deposited the leftover bones from their modest roasts. Then he washed his face in a bucket, gave me a slap on the back and left to sign the timesheet.

Let's say it was November. At that very moment, an unearthly scream coming from the bathroom shook the whole block. It was Violeta Jurado, whose last squirt of piss had revealed a rat, drowned in the toilet. We'd been trying out a new poison that drove rats mad with thirst, because everyone had run out of ideas of how to stop them. A fat matron rat had once fallen on Violeta's typewriter as she worked on the Director's novel. The rats were so out of control that we were always trying something. We even got to the point of buying a ferret once, but it ended up mating with the rats and the results were so monstrous that we went back to poison.

Violeta Jurado's scream caught the attention of Nacho's daughters, who came out onto the terrace intrigued. Because he couldn't leave them alone he always brought them with him to work. I think the poor girls didn't particularly enjoy themselves at the Ateneo, where they only had Ingrid's Pomeranian to play with, but it must have been worse for them to stay in the boarding house room. Nacho hated to see them so bored and he realised they were becoming unhappy. One day, so he told me, he had found them in their room watching the volume control signal on the television. It was seven in the morning. The two of them were sat on the floor, leaned up against the bed with their night dresses stretched down to their ankles, hoping that the programme would start any minute. Nacho covered them in kisses and swore never to leave them alone again.

Since then the girls practically lived at Ateneo Neruda. They seemed nice and they even came in handy for making up the numbers of the audience at lectures. This was the Ateneo's eternal problem. When the speaker was one of the Director's mates, the staff would pack out the auditorium, but that meant everyone else at the Ateneo was left adrift. Nacho's girls fell asleep on the chair and he took the chance to slip out. Later, during the toast, you could see the girls alone behind the nibbles.

One day Nacho came back very late to collect them. The pair were asleep on the floor, smeared up to their eyebrows, sleeping soundly next to the remnants of a chocolate cake. 'Aren't they divine?' said the lecturer's wife. 'Just a shame they have to grow up,' replied Ingrid Romero. We helped Nacho to carry them into the street and put them on the motorbike. We settled one on the petrol tank and the other on the back seat. It was an old Puma that you had to pedal to get started. The smaller one gripped onto Nacho's bomber jacket for dear life as he pushed off into the street with his feet. He seemed like a wading bird about to take flight. I waited on the pavement until they turned the corner.

Violeta was beside me, blowing her nose. She watched the motorbike disappear with a glazed expression, and then we

29

went back inside. She'd lived for the girls ever since she'd been after Nacho. A fortnight ago she'd organised a party for their birthday. In those days birthday parties happened at home and not in any old McDonald's. The girls were excited. Violeta prepared a big pot of chocolate and egg yolk sweets, and later she organised apple-bobbing and a sack race. She served up their chocolate on a special table and they drank it with Nacho. Whenever I see a little girl drinking something next to her father I remember that time at the Ateneo. They were called Natasha and Tatiana, but people got them mixed up.

Violeta was the chief of Cultural Action. Now I understand what a feat that was. She had started at the Ateneo with her Physical Expression Workshop, which quickly became a success. I can still see the mothers plotting during the class. They spent hours in the corner, constantly pestering their daughters. Every now and again a girl would go over to the group with her bun undone, or half-drenched in tears because she couldn't get her pirouette right. Her mother would give her milky coffee from a flask, while telling her off under her breath and throwing suspicious glances in Violeta's direction.

Violeta dreamed of putting on *Sleeping Beauty*. It was a difficult project that sent her half-mad. The only prince to hand was Yupanqui Varela, and although he was an excellent malambo tapdancer, he lost all grace when it came to Blue Bird. His entrances colliding with fairies or ghosts had become infamous, as had his failures in lifting. Consuelo once went headfirst, and he knocked four teeth out of another one. You can imagine the mothers' terror when Yupanqui appeared on stage. They begged Violeta to replace his role with bits of *Coppelia*.

Violeta had nerves of steel. She persuaded the man from the workshop to play the footman and Nacho's girls appeared as snowflakes. She never did manage to neutralise the hostility of the mothers; they plotted shamelessly. The ringleader was a retired star of the Regional Ballet, Ingrid Romero's cousin. This gave her free rein to criticise Violeta's every move mercilessly. However, much like Ingrid herself, the biggest role the cousin had ever played throughout her career was 'villager', although it once fell to her to understudy Coppelia, and she danced the whole piece with an idiotic expression, as if she was reading a book but without ever turning the page. Violeta faced up to the mob without losing her composure. Apart from the mothers and people like them, everybody fell in love with her. Her legs were the envy of any ballerina, and the same could be said for the rest of her. I suffered just thinking about her body, draped like a swan's shadow over Nacho's mop of hair.

Ever since Violeta had taken the Cultural Action job, Ingrid Romero had started to harass her. She wasn't about to let any old hussy rain on her parade. She had been at the Ateneo for ten years without taking a single day off sick, she revealed at the top of her voice. Violeta's ascent was ruining her personality and she began to fall out with everybody. Soon an unstoppable rumour started to spread: Ingrid Romero was a lesbian. This wounded her mortally.

We were playing cards one evening when the door was opened with a loud kick and she came into the library screaming:

'So I'm a dyke then am I? Who's the son of a bitch who's been going around saying that?'

She was brandishing the curved blade that we saved for carving the suckling pig at New Year. We all jumped backwards, shitting ourselves. I've never seen people as terrified, even though not just anyone came to the Ateneo. It was a bolthole for out-of-work ministers, legislators who'd been laid off and even policemen under investigation. If needs be, any son of

State would seek refuge here. They were dubbed mutants, and the mutant influx happened either at the end of the year or after a military uprising. That night with Ingrid there was only one new mutant, but he jumped off his chair with such reflexes that you would have thought he'd spent a lifetime at the Ateneo. We were finally saved by the ex-ambassador to Haiti, who ended up with the knife in his hands and Ingrid sobbing in his arms. 'Me, a dyke...' she murmured, hurt, while she counted up all the willies she'd offered sanctuary to in her long career.

The Ateneo was so brimming with staff that we accepted the new night rota without saying a word, which meant that we had to stay until seven the next morning. The audience wasn't particularly healthy at night; in the reading room there was hardly anybody, at any hour of the day. Our library wasn't like one of those ones in Philadelphia that you see in the movies, where detectives go to solve murders. The books were covered in administrative dust, mainly legal journals or old medical treatises donated by widows who were moving house. Along the bookshelves you could see all sorts, from jugs with little spoons in and electric heaters to cleaning tools or Ingrid's tortoise. But one thing we did have was a little workshop manned by the One-Eyed Florentine, who was actually blind. He worked away in a corner of the library, carrying out little tasks like mending a plug or sticking a chair back together. Sometimes, when we were playing cards, we could hear the murmuring of his work. When our shift was over we left the library, but he stayed inside. The last one out switched the light off. I could never get used to it. 'You turned the light off on him!' I yelled the first time. Nacho looked at me oddly. 'But he's blind...' he said. His irrefutable logic shut me up, but I still always felt the same as we left the library a little before dawn. One-Eye said goodbye to us with a smile as if he was just waiting for us to turn the switch, otherwise I'm sure he would have warned us immediately, 'The light!'

Now that he was dancing in *Sleeping Beauty* we all saw him in a new light.

With Violeta in Cultural Action things started to turn around. Nacho dusted off the old projector and we started a season of films. First was *Casablanca*, planned for the whole weekend, but the projector broke during the first showing on Saturday. The theatre was plunged into darkness halfway through the film. I'd had a bad feeling from the moment the projector had started to shake. It was just as Ilse said to Rick:

'With the whole world crumbling, we pick this time to fall in love.'

To which Rick responded:

'Yeah, it's pretty bad timing. Let me see. Yes. They were putting a brace on my teeth. Where were you?'

'Looking for work.'

Just then a cannon thundered, drowning out the projector's squeaking sounds.

'Was that cannon fire?' Ilse asked, after kissing him passionately. 'Or was it my heart beating?'

And then the projector died. There was an ominous silence and then the theatre lights came on. Right in the middle of the best bit, I sighed. People grumbled in their seats. My stomach was hurting. They were a dangerous and difficult audience. We once had to cancel a theatrical performance because they were swearing at the actors. Now they were nailed to their seats. 'I'm going to tell them how it ends,' whispered Nacho, who had reappeared in the chair. But the bastard had spent half the movie getting out of it in the bathroom, so he didn't even have a clue what we'd been watching. He told me to lend him a hand. How are you supposed to sum up the crux of *Casablanca* in a few seconds? I did the best I could, until Nacho got up, crossed the stalls in two leaps and positioned himself, microphone in hand, right in front of the screen. And now for the equipment to break, I thought. The microphone usually packed up, but miraculously it worked. Without further ado, Nacho launched into the plot. There were only remnants of *Casablanca*, but the audience seemed satisfied. Thank God that the plot had at least rung a bell for Nacho, like the fact that Rick ran a bar in Morocco and there was a black guy on the piano. He only made a few alterations, like turning the black guy into a member of the Resistance. After beating the Nazis, the black guy's mates captured a few of the Luftwaffe's planes and parachuted into the French countryside. This seemed a great opportunity for Nacho to sing the Marseillaise. As well as being in tune, it was particularly good for action scenes, so that Nacho soon had the audience eating out of his hands. Violeta seemed touched by *Casablanca*'s new brilliance. The mutants didn't skimp on applause, while we begged for the microphone back.

The problem was that the sound would screw us over too. Once, with Borges himself at the lectern, the microphone cut out unexpectedly. You couldn't hear a thing, but he just kept on talking. Nobody dared to interrupt him, and there were even several rounds of applause. Borges never even realised. Nobody really minded; it was just good to have him there on an autumn evening, broken microphone or not. But Nacho wasn't Borges, as Ingrid Romero kindly pointed out.

The people who really benefited were the deaf, who spent the next month discussing the lecture. In the Inventory Department there was a deaf couple who were always arguing. They were the only Ateneo employees in a relationship. We were used to seeing them arguing in the theatre, but this time it went too far. It must have all started because of something Borges had said. It was dinner time. Words flew back and forth and their tone was getting more and more heated. Soon they were saying horrendous things, until the deaf man thumped her. She wasn't in the least bit cowed and carried on the argument from the floor. She made gestures like *this* and *that* with her fingers, which sounded like a rather serious insult. Her boyfriend demanded that she repeat what she had just said and she spat right at him. What crazy slanging matches deaf people have. Just as he was about to finish her off, the deaf girl kicked him right in the nuts. Then he dragged her by her hair and it was then that Violeta stepped in. The next day they were as right as rain, eating their sandwiches and chatting away to one another.

Later she got up to go to the bathroom, leaving a trail of hormones behind her.

'What a backside,' said the One-Eyed Florentine, with his infallible sixth sense.

'If only she could talk,' said Nacho.

I'll never forget the deaf couple, reading Borges' lips in the stalls of the Ateneo.

So Violeta ended up becoming very well established in the post. Not even the band of mothers managed to topple her. Now she steered the Cultural Action department with a steady hand. It all started to go to the Director's head. He started throwing promises around left, right and centre that, with an increased budget, the dance school would become the Argentine Bolshoi, or so he said to his deputy. The truth was it was still lacking. Yupanqui Varela was still doing his lifts as though he were shouldering sides of beef in his job at the meat-packing depot. Anyway, the mothers could do whatever they wanted as long as their daughters were enrolled in the Physical Expression Workshop. This did nothing to improve the relationship between Violeta and Ingrid Romero. Her actions proceeded to take a turn for the worse. To annoy Violeta, she would burst in in the middle of a class in leather sandals and rollers and start practising at the bar. Meanwhile, the mutants didn't stop winding her up. One day a freshly butchered kid goat appeared in the freezer. It was the same week that the Pomeranian disappeared. Her dog had been missing for twelve hours, when Ingrid had a panic attack, until the mutants released him. Despite everything, these problems didn't manage to undermine Violeta's spirit.

Nevertheless, everything came crashing down in one go. It all began, I believe, with a hidden .38 that turned up amongst the books. Someone took it upon themselves to call the police, so we soon had the Chief of Police in the Director's office.

The Director, as usual, still hadn't arrived. I entertained the Chief as best I could, while Ingrid made coffee. The .38 was on the table, with bullets in the chamber. I mentioned last year's robbery to the Chief. A bank had been held up in our block. People had always said that the thieves had managed to get away through the vaults of the Ateneo. What if somebody had taken the opportunity to get rid of the weapon? I suggested. Anything's possible, nodded the Chief, but he didn't seem to want to enter into a debate with me about it. He wanted to know if we had a grammar book for his ignorant son instead. Could he take it on loan? Until November, if possible.

I agreed straight away, while trying to expound lengthily on our cultural work. Something told me that I should keep the Chief as far away from the .38 as possible. I didn't have to try very hard. All of a sudden the Chief's eyes clouded over as a contortionist rat came travelling down the curtain. It was a nocturnal explorer, but the evening was only just drawing in. They had no respect for the time of day any more. Maybe the situation above had got worse. All the rats in the area lived up there. At night we could hear them scuttling around, but we were actually fairly oblivious to what could be going on in the ceiling. We had sealed off almost all the exits and only the smallest ones ventured down, like this typical explorer. At least that's what we hoped.

The rat passed by us with real confidence, then disappeared in the direction of the bathroom. They say that rats always stick to walls, but this one crossed the office. The Chief seemed tempted to blow him away with a single shot. From then on we talked about nothing but the rats. I painted the situation in a few words. The Chief gave me his card; he knew a company that exterminated rats electronically. I promised I'd call. Then I told him about the ferret. We had let him loose in the ceiling in desperation. We never laid eyes on him again, but we harboured certain theories about his destiny. It was just possible that he had become the alpha male. After all, it did sound different up there. I'm not going to say like hippopotami shagging, but they definitely weren't rats either. So much so that Ingrid decided to take a look. She leant the ladder against the wall and went up with a torch. She peered into the cracks and came down with a strange look on her face. She hadn't seen any evidence of the rats, but she had seen *something*. I remembered that at the time we had considered putting a pair of ferrets to stop the male from going around falling in love with the rats. But in the end we had decided against it. Someone had told us that there was no hope. The One-Eyed Florentine, if memory serves. The female wouldn't last five minutes. A rat would do anything to seduce the ferret.

Now, while I was chatting to the Chief, I put forward a new theory to explain the matter of the revolver. Maybe it was a case of legitimate defence. Everybody was feeling stressed and anything could jump down from the roof. It may just have been for shooting rats. The Chief agreed, without wishing to continue the discussion. Then the Director arrived, bowing obsequiously. I had to get out of the office.

Ingrid Romero was outside.

'What was it?' she asked me.

'Nothing. He wanted to know about the revolver.'

'And?'

'I told him it was probably something to do with those bank robbers.'

Ingrid smiled scornfully.

'And why not?' I said.

She shook her head.

'You're even more stupid than you look,' she groaned.

The revolver was Nacho's. I heard it from his own mouth, a few minutes later.

For once, I saw him genuinely upset. We were in the kitchen together, making *maté*. Nacho looked pale. He'd just got to the Ateneo. He hadn't heard about the police being inside until late. Officers everywhere. I stuck my head out of the window, which overlooked the stalls, full of empty bottles. There was an officer stationed at the foot of the dividing wall, examining the flowering climbing-plant with interest. You could see that the guy was mad about plants. A few steps away Natasha and Tatiana were tormenting the Pomeranian. Two mutants went by in front of us with a trolley-full of books. It was an excuse to survey the lie of the land. Nobody wanted to miss a thing. The mutants were worried that the cops were after Nacho. I started to think so too. He even said to me, 'I feel like they've been following me.'

So it didn't really take me by surprise. Deep down, we all had our hunches about Nacho Alcorta. He was the only one in that pigsty that still kept his faith in the Revolution alive.

'And now what?' I asked him. It seemed to me that we should get him out of the Ateneo as soon as possible. But what could he do with the cops on his back?

Nacho didn't let his girls out of his sight. He muttered:

'What am I going to do with the girls…'

'Leave them to Violeta,' I told him.

Nacho shook his head.

'She's involved in it all too.'

'It' was the armed struggle. It was the last thing he managed to say. Shortly afterwards they took him away. We watched them disappear into the distance from the doorway, inside the police car. Violeta and the girls went in the other car.

'I hope they don't torture him,' said one of the mutants.

'No,' mumbled the ambassador. 'He's a political prisoner.'

'And since when don't they torture them?'

'Why don't you leave it?' said Ingrid Romero.

For once she didn't shout. It was almost as if she cared about us.

'Nacho is a liar. He didn't go with the Tupamaros, he didn't fight Pinochet or anything like it. He's a petty thief, you understand? He's been going around robbing department stores for three months. He even robbed my cousin.'

'The retired star of the Regional Ballet?' we asked. Indeed, the very same.

'Why are you staring at me like that?' continued Ingrid Romero. 'She was the one who reported him to the police. She recognised him through his balaclava and everything. And do you know what? He used the girls as a cover. That's why the people in charge always let him in. He left them on the ground floor and went up with the gun. Goodness knows what story he'd tell the poor little ones.'

One could already picture the scene. Nacho was capable of transforming every robbery into a marvellous story. The girls waited downstairs as if they were playing Hansel and Gretel. Later they'd get ice cream. I didn't dare ask if Violeta was part of the operation too.

It was completely dark. We were still on the pavement. Even the One-Eyed Florentine had come out into the street. Somebody spotted Nacho's motorbike and we decided to bring it inside. We all went back into the Ateneo, behind the motorbike and Ingrid. The ambassador came with me.

'He told me he had been in Bolivia in one of Che's camps,' he confessed.

I didn't say a thing. At that moment the Director went by with the Chief of Police, who was carrying the secondary school grammar book.

That was two hundred years ago. Nacho never came back to the Ateneo. They say that when he got out of prison he managed to be made Tourism Secretary. That was in the North, I suppose. That was when he started building up his business. He began exporting meteorites and other things from the sky. He soon expanded his catalogue. He was the first person, apparently, to put a dinosaur footprint on sale. Lately he'd turned to cave paintings. But he'd made a fatal error. To attract tourists he had no better idea than to go around spreading petroglyphs all over the sierra, which turned the region into the worldwide capital for cave paintings. He couldn't see a cave without going in to decorate it. This meant a flood of subsidies, but in the long term it cost him his head. From then on we lost all trace of him. I never thought I'd end up meeting him again in the old setting of the Cold War, selling bits of wall amongst the Turks and the Russians on the bridge.

I paid for my beer and I slipped out through the open air tables, past middle-aged fräuleins devouring *Cremetorten*. Suddenly I found myself on the bridge. It was the time of day when the tourists start leaving Oberbambrücke. Nacho was serving some English woman. He gave me a smile when he saw me next to his stall, while he explained to the English woman the suffering of his family during the worst of Stalinism. The girl listened to him, spellbound. Soon Nacho was telling her about the part he played in the collapse of the Wall. He showed her a photo too. Meanwhile he said a couple of words to me to keep me waiting, without giving any sign of having recognised me. I decided to have a look at his merchandise. There was everything from an old samovar to secret KGB documents about UFOs brought down on Soviet soil. Everything had a high sheen, like it was recently manufactured in Malaysia. Finally I went for the pocket watch with the KGB crest. I only had a big note. Nacho took it with indifference. His enthusiasm had melted away with the last tourist. Then he called to his daughter. It was Tatiana, I'm almost certain. She was a few metres away, basking in the Berlin sun. She left her little baby daughter on the ground and came over with the change. Her eyes passed over me as if I were oxygen, then became lost in the waters of the Spree. She was half stoned or something. 'Violeta's on her way,' she said to Nacho when she came back with her baby. She said it in the hard Argentine accent of Buenos Aires. I could just about make out, fleetingly, a woman in a fur hat coming over the bridge. Violeta was one of those women that you only find in magazines, that have to bend a little to kiss you on the forehead. I recognised her instantly. I took the change without counting it and set off towards the other side. I soon heard footsteps. Tatiana came running with the watch in her hands. After all that I'd left it on the stall. It'll never work anyway, I thought. I carried on down the Oberbambrücke as if it were towards the West. I soon went past the middle of the bridge. It was there, if I'm not mistaken, that the checkpoint with the barrier and the soldiers with helmets and rifles used to be. It was that bit in movies where the searchlights came on and the spy kept on going, with one foot practically in the West, but still at risk of being sprayed with communist bullets.

I saw Ingrid Romero again not long ago. She's doing better than you would have thought. I told her about my encounter in Berlin. She smiled sadly. She is still in love with Nacho. She still works at the Ateneo Neruda, although she should have retired. She is the Director of Cultural Action. The Ateneo has got its old name back, after spending a few years as the Gabriela Mistral Centre. The blind guy died a little while ago. Instead of the Pomeranian there is a cat. They're still called mutants. The jasmine keeps on growing.

'What can I tell you?' said Ingrid. 'Everything is the same. Even the little nest in the attic.'

She meant the bed and dressing-table and everything that Nacho had set up above the ceiling. It seems that Nacho and Violeta enjoyed it daily. It had hidden access, through the attic above the kitchen. It's now public knowledge and half the Ateneo uses it, even to have a siesta. The mutants play cards up there. At times when there are riots people who live far away can stay there for the night.

All in all, it's not a bad life.

Soul Radio

When the military surrounded the town and the race was cancelled; that's what I'm talking about. It was after midday. The street plunged into a deep coma by the sun's glare. Not the slightest breeze. You could have heard a fly yawn. The three of us sat on the pavement as usual. In barely a handful of hours we had aged a hundred years. We were opposite the house, chewing over our bitterness, when we were encircled by that humming sound that soon grew to a roar. As it did so, there was a gear change that stole our breath away. Choclo Sosa's Pontiac? It sounded more or less like that when it skidded after braking sharply. It was coming from the other direction. Judging by the roar, it had done the last forty metres sideways, its wheels smoking. Revving too high, its exhausts rattling and about to blow a gasket. We smelt burnt rubber. We imagined him rounding the corner, the nose already lined up straight down the road, the road the house was on, the usual route the Grand Prix took when it came to La Punta.

But we saw no such thing. The only thing that came into view was Cachencho in trainers, who came gripping the steering wheel with his eyes to the ground, shrouded in a cloud of dust and spit, his face bright red with the tension of driving. Cachencho, all signs seemed to suggest, was leading the Grand Prix. He had glasses on. They were welders' goggles that he'd found in the street. Cachencho was only wearing them for the Grand Prix. These days he drove nothing but the Pontiac. He spent the rest of the year turning everyone deaf with the first thing that came into his head. It could be a Scania truck packed with cows or the TAC super executive sleeper. But that deadly afternoon it was the Pontiac Catalina done up by Choclo Sosa.

Cachencho lived right by the house, so you could hear him as soon as he set foot outside the door. At times the illusion was perfect. *It was* the Pontiac Catalina crawling through Dog's Pond; *it was* the ambulance heading out to some violent disaster; *it was* the governor with his convoy of nine motor-cyclists. It was all about keeping Cachencho out of your field of vision. His ambulance, for example, was a masterpiece. Not only because you could hear it from six blocks away, but be-cause it sounded more tragic than a real ambulance.

During the Grand Prix, Cachencho couldn't keep up. He would get wound up straight away. They hadn't even set off properly from Buenos Aires before he was running about all over the place in the Pontiac while we were tucked away in my house, glued to the radio trying to decipher the race from the sounds of the Universe. We listened to Radio El Mundo. You could only catch it, as it happened, when it collided with Radio Escudero, our local station. But that fateful siesta, the airwaves were full of nothing but speeches.

So it was that we were sitting there on the pavement, defeated by misfortune, when Cachencho went down a gear and appeared on the corner. My bitterness intensified just looking at him. The Grand Prix wouldn't touch La Punta this time. We'd woken up to that bombshell. Not satisfied with capturing the town, the soldiers had just declared it capital of the Republic. Now loyalist aircraft were threatening to bombard us. It was because of this that the Grand Prix had been diverted. The first time in history it wouldn't pass by the house. On top of that, we had to put up with Cachencho, who came screaming round the bend. What could we do, given the circumstances? Well, pelt the twat with stones, which we did with enthusiasm.

Cachencho disappeared into the distance with his back wheel screeching and the fan belt about to snap, which came out just right. We were still impressed by him. We had finely tuned ears, the product of years of listening to races. Even in the middle of the night we could tell if an engine going by was this one or that one. 'It's Choclo Sosa,' one thought in bed. 'He's creeping round Dog Pond.' And it would be none other than Choclo and he'd just swerved past the pond. Or it was the Camarenas' Fiat with its loose exhaust pipe, or the runaway Chevrolet headed for some ditch or other. But compared to Cachencho, we had our ears up our own arses.

You had to be there when Choclo started the Pontiac up at the back of his house, which he used as his garage. Half the town would gather, even on chilly nights. Choclo would play with this and that and get it going again. There were benches and everything, on top of fuel drums and piles of useless batteries. It was a homemade amphitheatre, and we turned up to the putting right of the Pontiac as if it were a concert. Only Cachencho stayed closed to Choclo, ready to hold up the lamp or pass him a key.

Cachencho didn't exactly work like clockwork. Choclo could have got it done more quickly getting the things by himself. Plus Cachencho was always dropping things. Choclo waited patiently for the forceps to be passed his way. Sometimes he drifted off and stopped asking for tools, with his torso buried in the engine. Then Cachencho would slip into the driver's seat of the Pontiac. He'd spend hours there, his body half twisted, looking through the rear window with one hand on the wheel and an arm on the headrest. Anyone could tell he was racing. It couldn't be anything other than the Tour of Algarrobo. Cachencho was mad about that one, the race that the Camarenas had to finish in reverse, the only gear left after they'd blown the gearbox. They went twenty kilometres across the mountains. The spectators themselves lifted the car into the air, gave it a half turn and set it back down on its new course. From then on, because of this, you'd see Cachencho running around the town backwards.

He was a lucky bastard, no doubt about it. Seeing him now in the Pontiac was more than a man could take. We would suffer from our benches consumed with spite, while the Pontiac growled increasingly smoothly, all of its juices flowing. God gives bread to the toothless man, one of my friends used to say. Of the three of us, I was the most buggered, because of the rumours going around about Cachencho that they never stopped rubbing in my face.

But nobody ever gave up their spot. If there was a heaven on earth, it was Choclo's garage. There were always a few big noses, sniffing around amongst the tyres and all the spare parts. There were crankshafts and broken casing piled up and old clutch plates hanging on the wall. They were all waiting for the scrap dealer, who would never take anything with him because Choclo wouldn't sell a single screw. His assistant cleaned parts on fuel drums with a bit of wood on top. Sometimes a whore would come by with a packet of croissants, but the most awaited visit was that of the sign writer. He would come the night before the start of the race to paint the meagre list of sponsors on the doors and roof. There was the Guareschi bakery and the service station. As there was never enough money, we had a raffle. Top prize was a bag of sugar and second was a voucher for petrol. We would go from door to door with a book of tickets. Now, thanks to the military uprising, all our efforts had gone to shit.

After Cachencho had passed by the pavement outside the house, everything returned to its rhythm. It was dead calm. The trucks didn't arrive, and there wasn't a shot to be heard. Only the clamour of the siesta. The Automobile Club didn't even set foot in the street. Or so we told the swine from the next block who would pass by every now and again with some dolled up girlfriend with eyes full of guilt. The Automobile Club seemed comparatively very sensible for not dragging his girlfriend in tow, moving quickly and purposefully as if he were on his way to deposit cash at the bank.

Suddenly, something happened. A squaddie appeared in the distance. He was coming from the Hotel Dos Venados, headquarters of the rebel soldiers. I thought of *Lawrence of Arabia*, that scene where the camel approaches at full gallop and seems like a ball of liquid through the desert heat. That's what this thing coming down the road towards my house looked like. He soon began to look different. We soon spotted the submachine gun slung over his shoulder and a few grenades hanging from his belt. We stood open-mouthed until he drew up in front of the house and his boots stopped a few centimetres away from us. Then he asked about the radio station.

Only then did life start to regain some meaning. We offered to accompany him and soon moved off together in a V-formation towards our goal. He was a man of few words. Lieutenant Colonel Whoever, Minister of the Interior. He had to take over the radio, or so it seemed. All of a sudden the horizon shifted. An untold sea of opportunities unfolded before us, including listening to the race from the studios themselves.

But there was never any respite in this grimy town. Anywhere else in the world people would have been knocked for six. I don't know, everyone would have spilled out into the streets, rumours would have abounded. It was as dead as ever here. No one even came out to look through the window as we went by in a fan shape as if we were combing the area. It's the same old story. The one time you get a hole in one, nobody's watching. Whereas if we'd been taken prisoner with chains around our necks, everyone would have been ready to spit on us as we went by. We'd have given our right arms for one of those sad idiots who spent their entire lives in the doorway to have seen us on our way to storm the radio that afternoon.

We met with no resistance on our way to the door. The guards cleared the way when they made out the Minister. The entrance was crawling with soldiers. They would salute any beret, but they blocked our way. The Minister entered quickly. He didn't even bother to thank them.

We were still just about reeling from the shock when he came back out five minutes later, his hands on his head, held at gunpoint by the soldiers. They put him into a patrol car and set off raising the alarm. He was the Minister of the Interior, after all. But the coup had failed. The rebels had fled in the early hours. Nobody had remembered the Minister. They left him sleeping barefoot at the Hotel Dos Venados. He was an impostor of course. But how were they supposed to tell? Everybody saluted him. All soldiers look the same. The rest only realised the mistake when he started to read his address. He was on the other side! Only then did they jump on him.

That was the last century, when we weren't afraid and we weren't in love and The Carretera Grand Prix was the only thing that made life worth living. It was the year that the soldiers surrounded the town and the race was cancelled. Nothing was the same after that. Because, amongst other things, Cachencho had given up the steering wheel. Now he is in a wheelchair. He was hit by a bus going the wrong way in the Scania full of cows. At least that's what the bus driver said. Just before the collision he'd heard a mooing sound. Livestock transport on foot was another of Cachencho's specialities.

Choclo's garage doesn't exist. There's a bingo hall where it used to be. Choclo works in a kiosk now. 'I've had it with races,' he'll usually say. Races ended up ruining him. A sixth place in ten years was the best result he ever got. Now he rents a room with a bed without sheets. He never did sell the Pontiac. Last year we marched in procession to Dog's Pond and left the car as an offering to the Virgin. Here's hoping his luck changes. For now the car sits at the side of the road amongst the cloths and other offerings that people leave. Nobody dares to touch it, because it'd be a sin.

When I leave the house, Cachencho is on the pavement. They take him out early in the morning and bring him back in for lunch. Since the crash with the bus he hasn't spoken a word. From time to time we take him for a spin round the block to see if he'll find his voice again. But not even that can get him out of the hole he's in. I could only make out a slight brightness in his eyes the one time we took him backwards down the road, as fast as the chair could go. For one moment he smiled and tried to twist his neck, as if he was a Camarena looking out through the rear window while reversing. The son of a bitch knew he was racing the Tour of Algarrobo. But my mother, who knows nothing about cars, has told us that she's going to cut our balls off if we ever do that again.

I might take him to visit the Camarenas so they can take him out for a drive. I told him yesterday. It was siesta time and for once in their lives my friends weren't around. Cachencho gets nervous just hearing them arriving. I took the chance to recount the story of the race where Choclo finished sixth. Cachencho didn't show any signs of life. Does he even know who I am? At home everyone still says that he has a vast memory. At Mass, as it happens, he always used to say out loud what was coming up, or rather what the priest was going to say in the next few minutes, generally screamed at the top of his lungs. In the end the priest asked if they could bring him in the evening, because he was ruining eleven o'clock Mass.

From time to time I look him in the eyes to see if I can find anything. Then I stick a piece of broomstick on his forehead and I act as if I'm listening. He definitely does like this. It was the method Choclo used to use to sound out the motor. I also ask him if he loves me. My mother tells me to leave him alone. Cachencho loves in a low frequency, too low for human hearts to detect. Who knows how much he understands of everything you tell him? Finally, I grab his hand and put it in mine. I leave it a little longer each time. For fuck's sake, Cachencho, I say. The bastard doesn't even look at me. But I feel calmer. It's only a matter of time. As my mum always says, I'd better keep getting used to the idea that Cachencho is my brother.

Lazy Days in Polynesia

The last real King left is called Taufa'ahau Tupou IV and he is the incumbent ruler of Tonga. To start with, he weighs 150 kilos, which could amount to quite a lot more were it not for the daily bike rides that he takes with a swarm of bodyguards trotting at his sides. Who knows why he bothers with them all. Unlike the cast of puppet monarchs that appears in the pages of the magazine *Hola*, *nobody* in the whole of Polynesia would dare to lay a finger on Taufa'ahau. His people truly love him, and it would never even occur to them that he is a bit on the heavy side. In Tonga, obesity is resplendence itself, and it signifies wealth. These days the King is slimmer – a few years back, doctors told him, 'Lose weight or die.'

It is curious that this monarch with cannibal ancestors (but who doesn't have a cannibal at home after all?, as they say in Montevideo) should today be one of the most exacting exponents of British education, capable of enthralling any South American with his Bolivarian quotations. This King has a dignity that emanates from his very poverty. There are millions of little terraced houses in Buenos Aires that look like the Winter Palace next to his little residence in Tongatupu.

His mother was just as robust as him (one metre eighty-nine, barefoot) and inspired the same veneration. Some Londoners can still remember when Queen Salote (that's how you say Charlotte in Polynesian) visited Buckingham Palace for the coronation of Queen Elizabeth and weathered a downpour without moving an inch from her open-air carriage, as she felt it would be uncouth to get out and run for shelter. By her side, stoically enduring the rain, was a short Polynesian man, perhaps her Prime Minister, who wasn't even allowed to look at her as she had forbidden it by law. 'And who do you suppose that is?' they had asked Noël Coward, a comic writer of the period. 'Her lunch, naturally,' replied Noël.

Apart from his four-door Mercedes, the King has no other vices. Rumour has it that he has the monopoly on the bats that doze upside down in the *casuarinas*[7] of the capital. They are double-breasted vampire bats (five to every one of us) that supposedly taste like chicken, although no one has actually seen a Tongan sinking his teeth into a bat.

The most eminent visitor to Tonga turned out to be William Mariner, who arrived as the cabin boy of the Port-au-Prince. He was one of the few to escape the massacre perpetrated by the locals when the English boat landed. Mariner, who had just turned fourteen, charmed the Tongans and quickly mastered their language. It was thanks to this English lad that the Tongans discovered the mystery of letters.

This came as a result of a disastrous episode. One day Mariner, apparently sick of captivity, wrote an SOS to be handed to the first boat to pass Tonga. Finow, the King of the island, intercepted the missive and showed it to another British captive, who felt obliged to reveal its significance. Mariner's message was simple: it begged whoever set eyes on the letter to take Finow prisoner and offer him in exchange for them.

Finow listened dumbfounded. He found it incredible that one could understand so much through such a crude device. He dragged Mariner in by his ear and ordered him to do it again. Mariner printed the name 'Finow I' in a painstaking hand. The King sent for the other Englishman from the Port-au-Prince and told him to look at it. When the Englishman said his name out loud, Finow looked at the paper in terror, and even examined the back of it. Finally he declared, 'But this doesn't look anything like me! I mean, where are the feet? How does *he* (the Englishman who was reading) know that *these little lines* are me?' For the rest of the afternoon Finow got Mariner to write out everybody's names for others to read them.

After a while, Finow believed he had finally unpicked the mechanics of writing, and he attempted to explain it in his own way. Through these scribbles it was possible to represent something that was already known by two people, called say the Sender and the Recipient of the message. He nearly fainted when Mariner corrected him: one could write *anything*, even if the addressee had no knowledge of anything. Faced with such a huge revelation, the King went up to Mariner and whispered into his ear the name of an old adversary that he had most opportunely killed. Mariner noted it down on the paper which was passed on to the other Englishman. He read aloud the name written by Mariner and Finow, as white as those people who turn white in books, fainted and fell to the ground.

Apart from these incidents of Tongan cultural life, Mariner's days ran into one another, from one killing to the next perpetrated by Finow that would invariably end in some prisoner being barbecued, a dish the cook alternated with another typical recipe in which the bloke was cut into julienne shreds and baked in banana leaves in the traditional style.

But the greatest anthropophagi in Polynesia weren't actually from Tonga, but rather from some neighbouring islands known as Fiji. These islands were called, precisely, the Cannibal Isles. We met a corpulent Fijian on the day that we flew from Vava'u to Nehiatsu. He was at the front of the queue, ready to get onto the scales. The needle stuck at 128 kilos. His friend slapped him on the back enthusiastically, as he burst with pride. It's hard to board a plane in the South Seas without at least one person being sent to the weighing scales. Nobody gets offended about this. Maybe the imposing Fijian might even have jumped for joy if he had been made to get out of the aeroplane for being too heavy.

The Tongans are the children of the last free Queen of Polynesia. They have stayed poor but dignified and they haven't lowered themselves like the Tahitians, who go around the islands showing off in their 4x4s. Tahitians can no longer navigate by the stars, but when it comes to comparing the prices of household electronics they have a clinician's eye.

Unlike Tonga, French Polynesia has lost its magic. Nothing can be further from the islands in the days of the Bounty than this branch of Paris where the tricolour has flown for the last century and a half. Now they have to get by without the bomb. The atomic tests ended up corrupting them. Although it sounds unlikely, the inhabitants of New Caledonia wanted to die when the nuclear tests were suspended in Mururoa. If it was up to them, the French could have kept chucking atomic bombs until their hands went numb. Anything not to lose their jobs.

We do the same thing, a Spanish guy who came sailing from the Balearics told me: we complain to high heaven whenever somebody tries to shut down the nuclear power plant in our town. The plutonium levels in Mururoa are obviously through the roof. The French left, but they left enough toxins behind to last the next two hundred years. Something about their bad manners has stuck around in the atmosphere. Whilst the Tahitians serenade you on arrival, henchmen from the immigration department demand you show your return ticket or failing that, pay up.

By contrast, the Polynesia of Tonga shines as brightly as it has ever done, without Club Meds or jumbo jets or anything. Tongans conserve their irrepressible happiness. They have an inimitable laugh. A pair of Argentines from Río de la Plata who were travelling around Polynesia once put on a circus act on the back of a bus just to hear it. They dressed up as a bearded lady and a man on stilts, decorated the bus with flowers and balloons and put on shows in the marketplace, at which the

Tongans would laugh uncontrollably as only they knew how. You could spend your whole life in Buenos Aires and you'd never hear anything like it. Nobody laughs like that in the Pampas. Tongans only become serious on Sunday mornings, when they go to worship dressed as Europeans. The missionaries have managed to convince them that this is the sort of clothing that pleases the Lord. It occurs to me that Our Father might prefer to see them naked.

Meanwhile the King continues to fight tooth and nail to stop foreigners from getting even an inch of his land. He is afraid that when he dies the property development sharks will take half the archipelago. There are one hundred and seventy islands, which if you think about it really isn't that many. Some of them don't trust the prince, who seems pretty vulgar and capable of turning Tonga into a shopping centre.

In Vava'u we made contact with the select group of sailors that come to the kingdom every year. As November gets closer they will have to make a decision: will they spend the typhoon season here or will they leave for New Zealand or Samoa? They're unlikely to go to Capri or the Aegean Sea, two places ruined by the sort of ignorant loaded tourists that stuff the harbours with their cruise ships and scare off the poor locals.

The Spaniard from the Balearic Islands bombards us with questions about the Río de la Plata. He is a typical sailing bum, with everything but the fleas. He understands that Buenos Aires is one of the world's few remaining ports that still has time for sailors in need. His eyes seem to cloud over when we confirm this fact. It's the first good news he's had all year. We wouldn't say that the sailor's club will be falling over itself to greet him, but we still draw him a map of the route to Puerto Madero. He is disappointed to hear the following: don't even think about fishing in the Plata. Someone had told him that our waters were cobalt blue with white sand at the bottom, but now he's just found out that if he even splashes a single drop he'll have to have a tetanus jab. The Balearic Islander is crestfallen. He keeps searching for something reliable; he's been living off the hunt for a beer and any old fishing for six months now.

His boat is on its last legs. It's doubtful that it can even cast off from its moorings again. Maybe it's not even a sailboat anymore, but a marine elephant that came to Vava'u to die. Other boats are very ostentatious, but nobody knows why they come.

One evening we are anchored with No Name at a perfect bay that appears despite the bad luck. Against the backdrop of an impressionist's dusk, two boats from New Zealand arrive and drop anchor about a hundred yards away. They're playing bad rock music. For the next twelve hours the concert skirts around the one thousand decibel mark. They stay up all night and we don't get a wink of sleep. At nine in the morning, without even taking a glance at the landscape or the wildlife that surrounds them, they raise the anchor and set off with the music at full blast.

They nearly cut a little English yacht in half. A drowsy girl gazes out at them from the cabin, her eyes half-closed. Later she comes up on deck, starts to lower her bikini bottoms, nestles her divine backside onto the prow and wees shamelessly into the South Seas.

The shock of silence lasts a good while. The No Name is very peaceful. María puts her snorkel mask on and hurls herself into the depths. Paola grabs the little dinghy and starts to row towards the reef. We swim to the shore with Rafael to look for some coconuts. Coconut milk is so pure that the US Navy medics used it during the Pacific War for intravenous drips. Later toffs with yachts saved themselves from having to put up with the islands thanks to the coconuts that ricocheted around their radar screens.

Halfway to shore we spot a giant shell and we dive down to have a closer look. From below, we can clearly make out the No Name's hull about fifty metres away, its anchor buried deep into the sand. Suddenly a cloud of petals bursts out from the back of the boat and is silhouetted against the light like a snow storm falling over the coral garden. It is so beautiful it takes our breath away. It takes us a while to realise that it is the toilet's sluice. The white petals are pulverised loo roll. Somebody has just flushed the chain on the boat. A little way away, a sea bass eyes us bemusedly. 'He was the very image of Captain Cousteau,' Rafael will say later, when we are back on land.

A taxi driver is waiting for us there, and he drives like a man possessed through groups of terrified hens that miraculously manage to dodge out of the way. On top of promising us a bat stew, he also mentions that he can take us to the tomb of Captain Bligh. He is a very close friend of his descendants, who live in Noku'Alofa these days.

These tales about the Bounty still do the rounds throughout Polynesia. The taxi driver is lying: Captain Bligh died a long way from Tonga and he spent scarcely an afternoon in Tofooa, far too short a time to leave any ancestors, albeit in the South Seas. Bligh's so-called tomb really belongs to John Norton, another of the Bounty's crew left behind by Marlon Brando in a rowing boat. Tofooa, which lies in the heart of the Tongan archipelago, is a crater with a lake in the middle of it.

There's nothing more highly esteemed in the South Pacific than a good tomb. Stevenson was buried in Samoa. Gauguin is in the Marquesas. They say that on hearing about his death, the Polynesians cried, 'Gauguin is dead! We're ruined!' Captain Cook was buried in Hawaii and to this day his murderers' descendants still come to pay their respects to him. Cook died without knowing that in Tonga he had only just scraped through alive. Two local chiefs had decided to execute him, but because of some internal politics only half the programme was completed, namely the reception and the banquet. Cook left enchanted and even dubbed them 'The Friendly Isles'. He left gonorrhoea and syphilis behind for them as a parting gift. His surgeon was visited daily by Tongans who showed him their penises which were about to explode. It is well documented in all the books, whereas we'll never know on which jumbo jet we sent them AIDS.

And they are friendly, there's no two ways about it. One Sunday, while we are moored at Hunga, we receive an invitation to eat with Emeline Alu Hakalo at her Tongan shack. She serves albacore with coconut milk and a warm papaya salad on the side. We eat sitting cross-legged on mats, a position that rapidly becomes untenable. Our hostess chucks us a cushion and doubles up with laughter. Although we've taken to wearing the sarong, we haven't worked out how to sit like a respectable lady. Our shoes stayed at the door, on the inside so as not to be carried off by the dogs. Thousands of children are peering at us through the door. We are dying for a cold beer just as Emeline serves up this filthy looking concoction called kava, which is the colour of floor-cloth water and tastes like dental mouthwash. 'In Tonga, if it's not sickly sweet, then it gets you high,' the Balearic Islander told us. They even use some sort of vine as bait for fishing that makes the fish fly almost as soon as it hits the water, so that after they bite they start jumping around like Jim Morrison. There is another danger to kava: it would be no surprise if some people kept using it as they used to in the heyday when old men with better gobs spent all day chewing on the root and spitting it out into a bowl. Diluted with warm water, the paste turns into the best kava in the kingdom.

Hunga is a lovely place to stretch your legs after lunch. The town is surrounded by a cheap metal fence. The Tongans, horses, dogs and pigs live inside, and the vegetables are grown outside. Every family has its own little allotment that teems with gourds, coconut palms and yams, the patches sown any old how.

There is a horse in the distance. Along with a pair of lizards and some spider or other hanging in its web it seems like the only living creature. Not even the dogs, the skinniest, most humble dogs in the whole world, dare to set foot on the plantation. A scrap of the sea can be seen through the palm trees, ploughed by a single Tongan canoe that sails until Sunday ends.

Suddenly a sailboat comes into view, travelling along the coast. Hull encrusted with rust, sails covered in stains, a single man at the helm.

The lazy git from the Balearics!

He is listening to the match as he goes. He seems as down-hearted as those creatures that you see on the metro on a Saturday night, examining their knees on their way home, their dreams of Friday shattered. For God's sake, Paco, have a look at yourself. Somebody should remind you we're in paradise!

'There's a lot of desperation among us,' says Cora, a dark-skinned German woman who's not half bad on the saxophone, a crook with nice pins doing a round-the-world trip with her husband. In the evenings they both play a bit of music down in the cabin where other Spanish sailors sell paellas and tapas. They passed through Buenos Aires a few years back and met a couple of Germans travelling alone. The first one shot himself, and the second guy left his boat in Mar del Plata and never came back for it. And they seemed so happy, sighs Cora.

The problem with boats is that sooner or later they reach land, and it is well known, as Admiral Nelson once said, that boats and their crews stagnate in port. The Captain takes it upon himself to get us scrubbed up for shore, apparently pissed off with the mess and the obscene language used on board. The No Name will soon be sparkling, but the swearing will continue.

Whales come to Tonga to calve, although they don't arrive these days, so we console ourselves by taking the dinghy into a sea cave. Somebody comes out with a rude comment, surprisingly one of those members of the tourist mob tour group. These foreign sanctuaries have that sort of effect on people. The walls of the grotto sparkle, as well decorated as any public baths from Barcelona to the Bronx.

Is William Mariner's name amongst the graffiti, the British teenager who revealed the secret of writing to His Majesty Finow I two centuries ago? Will his name appear under the vulgarities tagged in aerosol by some drunk Australian? If he wrote that letter, he surely would have carved his desperate plea in a grotto. '*Help! Billy, 1807.*' Poor boy, educated the English way, if only his mother could have seen him. And not just because of the captives lined up in the baking tray with papayas in their mouths. What about the relationship between Mariner and Finow? Nobody gave freer rein to their appetites than the Polynesians, especially when it came to bisexuality.

Back at the boat I decide to do a bit of fishing. Marcelo and I hook unsuitable bait onto the wrong lure and cast it to the bottom on a line that's no good either. The fish are well aware of this and remain indifferent. There are millions of fish, in all shapes and sizes and not a single one is poisonous. Unlike in Tahiti and the Caribbean, where *ciguatera* is found alongside other deadly toxins, everything in the water here is edible.

Our fishing is in full swing, if you can call what we're doing fishing, when Engelbert Tofa Halakai arrives for his second visit. He pulls up next to the No Name in his hollowed-out tree trunk kayak. He is the island chieftain, or something like that. Next year, or the year after, or in ten years at the most, when it all becomes a shopping centre, he'll end up working in Hotel Paradise. For now he is the ruler of the island. He offers us breadfruit and we give him biscuits in return. The breadfruit is delicious. The Tongans throw them into the fire until they are completely charred, then take them out, peel them and eat them. It's like a thick purée. Captain Bligh's favourite little plant, which triggered the mutiny on the Bounty.

Night falls. Engelbert greets it with a story about his grandfather, who was once swept from his boat by a wave during a storm, and then swept back on board by the following one. We try to get him back with one about ghosts, but Engelbert's already heard it so we keep quiet.

Night on the South Seas. Silhouettes of coconut palms. What if we were to stay here forever? The only sound is the scraping of Beto's penknife as he whittles a piece of bone. As it seems that we've run out of things to talk about, Engelbert lowers his eyes shyly and says softly:

'Time starts here.'

He's right. Tongatapu is twenty minutes away from the International Date Line, the famous 180th Meridian. When he was still prince, the King suggested moving the time of the kingdom forward by one hour. His advisers leapt up, horrified: 'Dear God, what will happen to the lost time?' they demanded, close to tears. But the guy had the gift of the gab and he made a fair point: if they moved forward an hour, when the Universal Day of Prayer arrived, the Tongans would be the first in line to worship.

Engelbert was oblivious to political manoeuvring. Nor did he know anything about any old Meridian. But it seems to me he's not quite all there. He feels as though his island is slipping away from him and that in ten years, tops, he'll be washing dishes in Hotel Paradise.

Lost in the Desert

I'm going to pack my suitcase so I'm ready to leave good and early. I have to pack a few shirts and the Boongola hat that I brought from New Zealand. I've already turned the water off at the mains. Now I'm going to leave a note for the lady who does the cleaning, and then I'll lie down for a bit. What am I going to do with the cat after all? It's a perverse animal that doesn't even let anyone pick it up, but at the end of the day it does live in my house. I doubt I'll get any shuteye as I run through my journey in my head. Who told me to get involved in this? is the question I keep asking myself.

I'll think of that old primary teacher I guess, the one who made us draw exquisitely detailed maps of Argentina inside of which we'd put half of Europe. One had to take great care to fit in as many countries as possible. There was always some hole left for Portugal or Czechoslovakia and for Belgium and Denmark too. Once we managed to get twelve countries in there. The teacher, Miss Berta Chávez, was a dab hand at this sort of thing – she'd move the principality of Monaco, shuffle Greece and Luxembourg around and make space for another one. It was amazing that it all went in. If half of Europe fitted here and there was still some space leftover, how could anyone worry about the future?

What a disappointment it would have been if somebody had told us that it would take three countries like that to fill Brazil. But there was no danger of such an atrocity, as there were very few teachers in those days who would have dared to furnish us with a fact as subversive as that. It was back in the days of Juan Perón, when school was still an altar of patriotism. We were deep in mourning for Eva and every morning we'd observe a minute's silence and read from the manual that she had written for us. Then Miss Berta came up with her nationalist cartography. The longest avenue in the world crossed Buenos Aires, and the widest river in the whole galaxy was the Río de la Plata. The Iguazu Falls may not have been the highest in the world, but they were the most majestic. And do you know what? 'Poor Niagara,' murmured a North American politician as soon as he was shown them. We lived in what was practically the arse-end of the world, so you can imagine how astonished we felt faced with such revelations.

As soon as her repertoire of world records ran out, Miss Berta Chávez turned to the vastness of the Pampas. She said that only one hundred years ago the desert had come right up to the houses. It wasn't really a desert, but that's what they used to call the land ruled by the Indians.

In the times of the natives, an Argentine President was a cross between a general and a landowner, such that he completely understood the scale of the business. The conquest of the desert, if my old man is to be believed, was not much more than real-estate speculation with something of the police raid about it. But then again my dad was an anarchist professor who cursed God and the Virgin Mary with words so foul that I'd rather swallow my own tongue than repeat his diatribes. Miss Berta Chávez was as proud of her ancestry as she was of her magnificent bottom. I didn't want to torment her with my dad's cynicism, maintaining staunchly as he did that the whole conquest came down to a stroke of the quill, as the people linked to the government started to buy land up front that would later be stolen from the Indians.

According to the old man, that's how those cattle ranches that my teacher so admired came to be. For Berta, there were no words to describe them. At times they stretched right from the mountains to the coast and they looked more like a country than a smallholding. A family from Entre Ríos had a field with half a million cows, and in Patagonia there were ranches several times bigger again.

With such immense numbers, rounding up the herd could be pretty serious. Berta loved dealing with roundups on such a huge scale. Her grandfather had once set off for the mountains from the sea with a flock and he had only recently arrived at his journey's end eight years later, with his sheep's great-grandchildren.

So it was that my biggest obsession was those places that Berta drew. I may already have been thinking about my trip. I don't know when I got started on the idea. Nor do I know why I'm doing it. Why would it appeal to anyone? But I'm sure I was fantasising right from the start about those shadowy regions that used to border my house. It's strange though, that after all those years I never managed to write a single line about the desert, which so often kept me from sleeping.

It must have been a nightmare to hide in those places. Berta made us read a book. What an impression, crazy Sarmiento said, must be made on people by the simple act of fixing one's gaze on the horizon and seeing practically nothing. Because as they lowered their eyes in those diaphanous borderlands, they would be plagued by fascination and doubt. Where must this impenetrable world end? What is beyond the horizon? Loneliness, danger, death. Anyone who passed through there, he assured, would be so beset by nightmares that he would sleep with one eye open.

Well, I think I've summoned up the courage to go into the desert. I'll probably leave any minute now; I'm only hanging around because of this business with the cat. If I come back one day from those highlands, I'd like to celebrate with you. I don't know what I'm going to bring back from out there. It's better not to ask for details, and I don't even know them anyway. There are scenarios that I could share with you, that might not even matter at all, that I might not even bring back with me.

One of them is a single *caldén*, the sacred tree of the Indians that crossed the desert. Can I set the scene? The sun has just come up. A tree that seems to be blossoming appears in the distance, because every Indian that passes by leaves some little scrap of clothing hanging from its branches. It is very bad luck to forget this ceremony, so everybody always leaves something. And is that it?, you might ask. That's it. A tree with cloth flowers. It might not seem enough to set off to the desert for, but it's these little visions that make one leave the house, charge the antimatter tank and soar off to space.

The other scene takes place in the last years of the military expeditions, when a few soldiers go into the forests of Potrillo Oscuro where Pincén, the most rebellious of the *caciques*,[8] is hiding out. Although he will manage to give them the slip in the end, a pair of soldiers who are wandering around find a man more than a hundred years old, shrunk to the size of a sabre, stretched out on a few sheep skins, mummified but still alive. What could the poor men do in the face of such a discovery? Pick him up and take him with them, it would seem. One takes him in his arms, lies him across the back of the horse and carries him across the desert. They will have thought that the Indian would make them famous. They'll soon realise, however, that they can't go on with him. They don't even know what to feed to this shrivelled skin-and-bone creature that doesn't say a word and simply stares at them. They start to suspect that they have just made a mistake. They feel like those tourists who, having bought their fill of 'artisan souvenirs', realise at the foot of the plane that they won't be able to take them on board. The soldiers then dismount and dump the old man at the side of the path, and set off at a gallop.

It could be that these scenes don't mean a thing. Maybe I'll end up forgetting them. But they are the type of images that one needs to be able to dive deep into desolate seas. Only the hope of seeing a flowering tree in the middle of the desert can urge you to book the trip. I'd also like to meet that sabre-sized Indian that they tossed to the side of the road.

I've got another journey around the corner. I'm going to ascend to five hundred metres first, accompanying a friend who mans an observation balloon. This man contemplates from on high the dirtiest war that we ever endured. It lasted nearly as long as the Second World War. Back then, Paraguay was an honourable country governed by a psychopath. This psycho came up with the terrible idea of taking a riverside settlement from us. He was a sort of Argentine General throwing himself at the Falklands. Our troops ousted him in a single outing, and it could have ended there. We could have asked for diplomatic reparations, we could have demanded that they apologise to our flag: we could even have made a few pesos out of it. But instead we decided that we needed to save Democracy. As if the English, after taking back the Falklands, had decided to follow it back here. Our President had bragged in public, 'In the barracks in a week, on campaign in a month and in Asunción in three.' But even though we took the Brazilians along with us, and they had the fourth largest fleet in the world, a whole load of battleships and other boats like it, it took us five years to get to the capital, in spite of the fact that the Paraguayans fought barefoot. We razed the country to the ground and left barely twenty thousand Paraguayans alive.

It was worse than Vietnam. Brainwashed by the English, we massacred all of those beautiful people. After the war, there were more beggars than anything else in Asunción. Our shame became so great that we gradually abandoned the war so that by the time we took the capital we were reduced to one sad column that confined itself to watching the Brazilians sacking it from the other side of the river.

I am going to go up in this balloon to take a look from above. As it occurs to me on the eve of my departure, I am scanning the diaries of other voyagers, perhaps in search of some magic formula. A while ago I read that Arthur Miller no longer sat himself down in front of his typewriter to write a play. He just stayed in his chair in case it came to him, which is something completely different.

I'm going to open the door for the cat. He never loved me after all. My father was the only person in the whole world for whom he ever felt anything. When he died he got into his coffin with him and there was no way of getting him out. He only jumped out when he became aware of the fact that they were going to shut the lid. So I know that as soon as I open the door he will disappear into the night forever, and that soon afterwards I will lock the house up. I might leave the porch light on while I put on my Boongola. I'll grab my bag with my left hand to leave the other one free. Then I'll go out into the street.

I'm going to stand still for a while, until I get used to the shadows. The area has changed a lot.

I'm going to look left and right.

I might check once more to see if I've locked the door.

The same thing always happens.

I go round in circles because I'm scared shitless.

You know only too well how many people have never made it back from the desert.

You've Got to Die of Something

Then came the thing with my dad. They say you can't keep worrying about something that might never happen, but that doesn't apply here because I was going half mad from the moment that this whole thing began and in the meantime the problem just kept getting bigger, until they finally operated on him and it got way out of hand. My uncle and I had taken him right up to the operating theatre together, with the saline drip and everything. I mean we had both walked down the corridor a few paces behind the bed, me keeping a firm grip on my uncle. My dad suddenly announced that he wasn't going to get out of there alive. He'd been going on like this for hours, but everyone had ignored him. It's what happens with sick people. All they did was start eavesdropping at the door of the theatre. A nurse asked him how he was. Perfect, said my dad. But he wanted to tell them that he was going to die in the operation. Then they called the doctor, who bustled in noisily. Somebody told him that he should listen to my dad, to see if he really meant what he was saying.

'Do you know what you're talking about?' the doctor grunted between his teeth. My dad was suddenly apologetic, as if he was doubled up with embarrassment.

'Right, tell me what you said,' said the doctor.

'I've already told the girl,' the old man mumbled. The girl was the nurse.

'Well repeat it then man,' the doctor insisted.

He seemed pretty indignant. He had the mask on and everything, and he'd even got the gloves on already.

'Do you remember that we talked about this the other day?'

'Yes, doctor.'

'And what did we say then?'

'That the test results didn't look good.'

'No. What did I say after that?'

'That I was an ox…?'

'And?'

'That I can endure anything?'

'Exactly. Well, no one's life is guaranteed, but you're in perfect health.'

'Then I don't get why you're operating on me.'

'Yes you do.'

'Yes,' my dad nodded.

'Preventative medicine.'

'Yes, doctor.'

'A routine thing.'

'You're right.'

'And now you start coming out with this.'

The doctor looked worse than my dad now. He was still disguised as a surgeon with his hands held aloft so that nobody would touch them.

'What are we going to do then?' he asked him at last.

'You tell me,' my dad sighed.

The doctor decided to send him back. The auxiliary nurse who pushed the bed shook his head. You could tell that deep down he was over the moon and that he hated the doctor. My uncle and I joined the retreat, in the wake of the bed that was on its way back to the ward. 'That's why I never have any tests done,' the auxiliary told my father. 'They always find something,' he grumbled. 'If they open up your engine, you're finished.' He put the bed back in the room and we waited outside. Soon the doctor arrived to have a chat with my mother. She went out to speak to him in the corridor.

'I really am very sorry, but I just can't operate,' the doctor told her.

Tears pricked her eyes.

'Oh, doctor,' she sobbed. 'Why don't you let me talk to him?'

My mother had a blind faith in the medical profession.

'He thinks that he won't make it out of the operating theatre,' the doctor explained.

'But doctor. People have operations all the time…'

'He's not afraid. He simply believes that he's going to die.'

'I thought it was just a simple op?'

'Yes, well you could say that.

'And what if he doesn't have the procedure?'

'Then may God help me.'

'Oh doctor. It'd be better if you operated on him.'

'Look, I don't operate on people who come out with that sort of thing, because they always end up dying on you.'

My mother went back into the room and stood next to Dorila, whose boobs were now up to her chin. She was a dark copper colour. Dorila lived hopping between the sunbed and the plastic surgeon. She was family or something. I never knew how old she was and the only way to find out, according to my dad, would be to date her with Carbon-14. But I mustn't get off track. I'm sure that as soon as they got into the room they started trying to fill dad's head again.

In the end he surrendered, so we all set off towards the theatre again. 'Everything all right?' the doctor asked. 'Yes, very well,' mumbled my dad. They were mad if they believed he'd changed his opinion at all. He accepted so as to avoid an argument, like so many times before. Afterwards, he said 'See you later' to me. I went over to give him a kiss and his hug lasted longer than it should, which made me feel uneasy. 'Watch out for lorries,' he said, meaning on my bike. This was my last chance. I should have clung on to the bed, but I never would have done it – I was just like him in that respect; we both hated causing a scene. They wouldn't have taken him otherwise and I would have been spared those three interminable hours that

I had to wait in that room next to my uncle until the news came. My sister came to tell us in tears. We genuinely didn't know what to do. We saw the time on the clock tower outside through the window. It was only then that I realised that my dad was never coming back into the room. My uncle looked at his shoes. You couldn't tell if he was sleeping or not.

There were a few blackberries with cream left on the bedside table. They had brought them to my dad, but he hadn't even touched them. My uncle couldn't take his eyes off them. I put the plate in his hands. He didn't want to know, but I moved my head towards him, trying to convince him. Dorila must have found it revolting. It occurred to me that she'd be at home with us soon, and she'd make us all wear mourning, wouldn't let us watch telly and would make my mum cry the first chance she got. I tried to smile at my uncle, but I couldn't do it. All I wanted now was for him to eat the blackberries. I'd stayed firm on that point at least. If only I'd used the same strength of character to cling to the hospital bed.

My mother came in to take my uncle with her and I left the clinic. I bumped into the doctor in the corridor. Maybe I should have stopped to speak to him, but I went running out into the street instead. I jumped onto my bike and set off down the avenue, hunched over the handlebars. I passed by the house without stopping, then turned right and came out onto the motorway. There was a full moon, and it was pretty quiet. Every now and then a lorry would pass by blasting its horn at me. I kept close to the edge and gripped the handlebars tightly. I soon reached the mountains. By then I'd got over my breathlessness and I was pedalling better. I couldn't get the idea out of my head; I kept thinking about my uncle and the thing about the blackberries. My conscience was clear though; it would have been wrong to waste them. I wondered if my dad would have done the same.

I stopped at the top of the slope to look out over the lights of the valley. I needed a wee and I had a bit of trouble liberating my willy, shrunk by the cold. It was like having something that didn't belong to me in my hand. When we used to go out walking with my dad we would always stop around here. We would sit facing in opposite directions, focused and silent, and it was a special moment. That was a long time ago. Recently, before taking to his bed, he had gone out walking with my uncle. I'd bumped into them that night en route and had joined them for a stretch. My dad was recounting something to him as we went. Later we stopped for a piss. My uncle opened his legs and managed as best he could, struggling with his flies. It occurred to me that my uncle wasn't all that bad and it was a good thing that he was at home.

I'd reached the perfect rhythm with a smooth tailwind. I was concentrating hard and trying to keep my knees in alignment with my heels. My knees barely skimmed the frame. I imagined that I was in the middle of the péléton of the Tour de Sudamérica, stuck to the wheel of the guy in front, my arms hardly bent and the seat raised up as far as it would go. I thought that I might break away from the pack at any moment, shouting to the other cyclists to make way and parting them with both arms as I went.

I suddenly made a U-turn. I had an idea in my head. I needed to rescue a drawing that I had given to my father. He kept things he was given in an envelope, including my uncle's drawings, which might be made of old peelings or a dried up spider. I didn't want to see the others prowling about his bedroom, rummaging around in our presents. They'd emptied my grandma's wardrobe out all over the bed looking for a savings account book, which would have really hurt her. She would have shot herself on the spot. My grandma used to hoard things that not even my uncle would bother to keep. Her bedroom was stuffed with boxes full of medicines past their sell-by date, little religious tokens from baptisms, old bills, X-rays and blood tests, leftover wool, knitting swatches and the death notices of her girl friends. There was even a poem that my dad had dedicated to her as a boy. If she'd known she was going to snuff it so soon, my grandma would have chucked everything. I've still got the oven glove she gave me for my birthday. Everyone had a go at her because it was the last thing someone would give to their grandson.

Once I got home I went round the block a few times to see if the coast was clear. I didn't want to arrive right in the middle of the wake for everyone to turn and stare at me. But the house was in darkness. I waited on the pavement until the door opened and I saw my mum coming out.

'At last,' she sighed. My bike escapades sent her round the bend.

She looked me up and down quickly in search of any wound. Then she ordered:

'You stay at home with your uncle. There are some schnitzels in the oven.'

Then she hurried off to the funeral home to pay for dad's coffin.

As she was late getting back, we decided to go to bed.

My uncle soon appeared next to my bed.

'All right, but watch it, I don't want to wake up tomorrow all covered in piss,' I said, shuffling away to make space.

He got in and kept towards the edge of the bed. I was about to put my arm around him, but decided against it. I don't like to touch my uncle because you always get a sticky patch.

'Shouldn't we be crying?' he asked.

'I've already cried enough,' I told him. 'Now go to sleep.'

'Maybe I'll feel like it again later,' said my uncle, defensively.

'Why do you feel happier after crying?' he asked afterwards.

'You don't feel happy. Just calmer,' I explained.

'It takes the pain away?'

'More or less,' I said.

'That's what Dorila said.'

'Dorila's a bitch.'

My uncle changed the subject. Whenever he senses conflict he talks about something else.

'Did you know that a little girl killed herself to wait for her mum in heaven?'

'Did Dorila tell you that too?'

'They said it on the telly.'

Something moved at the foot of the bed. It was my uncle's toad.

'That bastard again?' I groaned.

'Leave him alone…'

My uncle had a toad that he had raised all its life and which followed him around everywhere. The toad never let him out of its sight. It would spend hours next to the chair while he ate his soup. It was a filthy creature. It gave you the urge to kick it along into the street, but I decided to leave it in peace.

'Leave it out with the sighing,' I said to him. 'It's impossible to live with somebody who sighs every twenty seconds.'

'I do not sigh every twenty seconds,' my uncle replied.

'How often do you sigh then?'

'I don't know.'

'Where did you get that bad habit from anyway?'

He carried on looking down at the floor, not knowing what to say. I decided he was all right really and ruffled his hair a little. Sometimes I get the urge to hug him, but I don't want to be thought of as queer.

My uncle is called Cristian. He has lived in the house since he was two months old. I think he's somebody's son. I wouldn't be surprised if his mother was Dorila, although I'm not sure if those sorts of old women can even have kids. Dorila is about thirty years old. Who's going to take him to nursery school now? My dad used to do that. I'll take him one of these days. If I manage to leave home, maybe I'll take him with me too.

Them

On top of everything else, they ransacked his house. It was his old den, the one in Calle Brasil, the same one he'd had for all those years. Nothing was further from this man than a black limousine or a presidential estate. They stole everything they didn't break. Someone had been obliging enough to ensure that his presidential sceptre and his private diary had fallen into the hands of a journalist, who was possibly his worst enemy. However, the latter put everything in a box and sent it back to the owner.

At the time, the President was to be found in a base, aged and feverish. He had sent a letter to the soldiers, offering his surrender. A captain came over to tell him, 'You can go wherever you wish, Sir. You are free to go.' The President, huge, afraid and feverish, sank down into his seat, and his memory had already buried itself deep in the minds of his tearful followers. Some of them had already started making deals with the rebel leaders. He raised his head and asked to be allowed to stay. In truth, he didn't have anywhere else to spend the night. He was no longer the President. Nor was he going to go back to a wrecked house.

To make matters worse it was possible, almost certain, that he was completely skint. He'd never taken his presidential wages for himself, and donated them religiously to the Sisters of Charity. He still had the same old habits from his time as a teacher, when he taught citizenship in a teacher training college. The girls were crazy about him. It wouldn't have been too surprising if a child had come out of it, provided that thing about the bastard children is true.

As a teacher, he was no great luminary. He never explained anything. How was someone who didn't even like giving speeches, who wasn't even a member of the party and who managed to hide away from the crowd at political functions supposed to explain something in a classroom? But he did like working as a teacher. If a girl didn't have a textbook he'd buy one on her behalf and give it to her via the headmistress so it would seem like it was provided by the school.

Now he was in the base, without a clue where to turn. Meanwhile, in the Casa de Gobierno,[9] *they* were still debating what to do with the President, whether to stick a couple of shots in his head or send him to a semi-deserted little island. They would, in the end, imprison him on a boat. For now, the official guard eyed him with curiosity. Why would he want to remain in the hands of his tormentors? Didn't he own any land? Hadn't he been a keen cattle farmer over winter? Why didn't he just go to his ranch?

In fact, he did have fields. The President, you could say, had been one of the two most exotic herders in all the Pampas. The other was Hermógenes Ramos, the only man who paid the Indians rent on the land. And what's worse, he was a heretic (that's to say a Protestant). His ranch was called Miraflores. If the Indians, who were pretty all over the shop, came to rob a calf from him in their confusion, they would leave it by the corral later with apologies for the mistake.

Whereas they stole everything from the President, right down to his cutlery in the raid on the house on the Calle Brasil. He had also bought his own fields; they didn't belong to the family nor was it land stolen from the Indians. He paid for his last ranch with credit from the bank.

But that wasn't the strange bit, as he would have paid it back. The loan came from the bank that had that outrageous collapse and ripped off all its savers. Neither lazy nor slow on the uptake, the bank's debtors rushed out to buy bonds at an unbelievable discount. Nobody was going to let that sort of opportunity go to

77

waste. No one that is, but the President, who arrived at the counter to pay the agreed sum. He was the only one that did so. You should always pay what you owe, he explained.

He wasn't one of those stereotypical well-heeled politicians who ordered their clothes from Europe and were lawyers at Lloyd's. His chambers were a stone's throw from the Casa Rosada. Who needed cannons now to overthrow a government? The President, on the other hand, was as far from heaven as he was from the World Bank. He always did everything back to front. He was a cattle farmer, but they booed him in the Ministry of Agriculture. He'd been a commissioner at twenty, but the police hated him.

Back then, when the President was wandering about in Balvanera with his commissioner face on, his friend they called the Gringo (another President in gestation) was jumping from whore to whore with his cronies, until he was denounced to the family by a neighbour. The neighbour in question was a midwife. To get his revenge, the Gringo dressed up as a woman in labour and an urgent call was made to the midwife. The trap was set in a friend's bedroom. There, in shadowy solitude, the Gringo writhed about between contractions in a blonde wig, well tutored by another friend who was a medical student. The climactic moment came as the midwife had to insert her hand to carry out the necessary manoeuvres, whereupon it collided at full speed with the Gringo's imposing thingy. If the midwife's screams were anything to go by, he was already well on his way to being Latin America's new macho man.

It's unlikely that the President was in the room at the time. He was always a lone wolf. He was one of the Gringo's best friends, but he didn't share in his pursuits. Nor had he been acquainted with the Gringo's parties where female choristers whose sole attire was a string of pearls around their necks would jump out of large puff pastry desserts. The President's family members were never really ones for parties. It is not even clear if he managed to finish school. He was the nephew of another politician called Leandro Alem. They say that the President had witnessed him shoot himself, toppled by depression and electoral failures. The President was in turn also the grandson of a terrorist, the infamous Leandro Alén (with an accent and without the m), who was hung in the square for having infiltrated a group of corrupt police officers. The family, out of sheer shame, decided to camouflage their surname.

People also wondered if the President was the bastard son of a certain bloodthirsty dictator, a rumour put about by journalists. We should remember above all of course that the newspapers couldn't stomach him. He had only just taken up office when they started to slaughter him for putting so many beardless men in his Cabinet. From then on there was no justice. They didn't even celebrate his little achievements, such as reducing external debt or protecting the value of the peso. That was the behaviour of almost the entire press, who ruled right up to the very end; the case might as well have been called 'Pen In the President'.

Now, nearly three years on from the revolt, the President lay dead in a distant region, almost as dishevelled as his ransacked house. The body was embalmed in a hurry. Permission wasn't granted to take him to Congress, so the wake was carried out in the living room. Nevertheless, his former entourage did turn up to the funeral. The crowd started to get wound up, and the chief of the squadron managed to keep his distance so as to avoid the people's anger. The guards seemed confused: didn't they have the right to accompany him to the grave? Well no, they didn't, but this made no sense to them. Nobody had explained anything to them. The truth was that *they* hadn't managed to solve the problem, not now nor in future. In any uprising they'd be faced with the same dilemma: what to do with the presidential guard, and how to stop them from defending him? It was no minor detail, as we're talking about a whole regiment. They would only manage to get them away from his side, so as not to have to kill them. That's why the guardian angels didn't carry out their duty and defend the President to the death. When the work was done, the guards returned to the scene of the crime, like those cops who go to have an awkward look at a deregulated zone. The man that they were charged with protecting had evaporated, and there was another in his place. That was all they could say.

It was the funeral of the century. The cortege travelled as far as the square and turned into a protest as it went. Lots of people would have liked his body to stay there forever, à la Lenin. But *they* had spread a rumour: employees that missed work that day would be fired immediately. This was a useless threat – the streets were crawling with people, but that was as far as it would go. The casket hit the ground three times, which *they* took to be an auspicious sign. The debut had been perfect; taking a country was easier than they'd imagined. They would take the reins as many times as necessary, without leaving men wounded or taking prisoners.

For now they are calm. They would stay there, lying in wait in a rented house a stone's throw from the centre of town, in a street with puddles and cats that leap in the shadows, watched over by an old lady who is paralysed by fear when she sees strange movements. She draws the curtains and calls 999, but no one has ever come.

Garrapatenango

They are two soul mates who whore their way through the town, fall in love with a girl and set off for Florida on rafts. That's the gist of it. It'll also be the tale of an attack on a West Indian resort by a handful of paratroopers from Guatemala who are defeated, flee in a boat, drift off course and end up as cannibals.

It's called Garrapatenango.

I can already hear you now, Grandma. 'Shit,' you're going to say to me. 'Can't you just tell simple stories about people like us? Something run of the mill. A love story?' Grandma, this one's swarming with people like us, starting with Juanjo Arévalo. What do you mean, Juanjo Arévalo who? My dad's teacher, who lived on the next street, in Lo de Videla, our neighbours for years, old family friends. When Juanjo was in La Punta, they put him up. I think he was reading under the grapevine when he received the telegram from the Caribbean offering him the presidency. I can just imagine the party at home. Of course you know who I'm talking about. You sent rain water for Juanjo's wife during the drought. Come on, Grandma, you love playing dumb. So what if your old man's teacher comes out one day saying he's the President of Guatemala? So what if his wife rinses her hair with the water from the cistern that you yourself send her?

Lo de Videla was the house with mynah birds and herons. Every year, towards the end of December, his cousin would arrive to spend the holidays, a skinny kid named Jorge who already had the look of a General about him back then. It's hard to imagine those two together, drinking *maté* on the terrace, Jorge Videla and Juanjo Arévalo. Who would have thought it, eh? Who would have predicted that the skinny kid from Buenos Aires would, in time, come to commit such atrocities, let alone all the stolen babies and people chucked from aeroplanes. And I don't know where to start with Juanjo, you probably know better than anyone. I wasn't there then. Nobody remembers him around here anymore. They took him to be a dangerous red, who left the women of the town all aquiver with his boxer's physique and kept in shape by drinking *café con chile*, which was the Caribbean name for red hot chilli sauce. My mum recalled him in his ranger's hat, coming back from the Institute with my old man. They said goodbye to each other in front of Lo de Videla and dad carried on home.

But his greatest friend was Mario. He was Juanjo's best friend in La Punta. When he became President, Juanjo brought him to Guatemala as his guest of honour right in the middle of the World War. On the day that Mario returned to Argentina, Juanjo gave him a gift and asked him to open it as soon as he had boarded. It was a box wrapped in yellow cellophane. The police suspected something was up as soon as Mario arrived at the airport. They took him to an interview room and made him unwrap the parcel. Mario's hands trembled as he ripped the paper. The police were burning with suspicion. They were convinced that there was SOMETHING inside. Mario lifted the lid steadily. The cops cried out in horror. Do you know what was in there? It was a dead bird, a stuffed quetzal. The sacred bird of Guatemala, about to be smuggled out by a foreigner, and an Argentine at that! Mario turned spinach green. A squaddie twirled his handcuffs around. Suddenly the door opened and Juanjo came in laughing his head off. The policemen joined him. Then the President squeezed him tight with a hug, and Mario finally realised that it had all been a wind-up set up by Juanjo, the delinquent of the Videlas.

So Juanjo was the head of my school? For me, the real head was Mario, who had taken over from Juanjo and would stop in front of us every day to say, 'Good day, children,' to which you had to reply, 'Good day Mr Headteacher,' all with deep mourning in our hearts because Evita had died. From time to time his female deputy would replace him, but the most incredible thing was when one morning, instead of Mario or the Deputy, it was my dad who came out to greet us. If you've ever felt like putting a bullet in your head when you're seen with your parents, imagine what it's like when the entire school is lined up in the playground to witness it. My dad was now the government-appointed head of the school and Mario was disgraced as a Peronist and nobody wore mourning on their lapels anymore.

Was it around the time of the Plateros? A bit earlier, maybe: the year that the Mulatas de Fuego came from Havana to dance in the Opera House. It was a windy autumn. On the way back from school we followed the tiny stream, trickling along beside the desert thistles. The donkeys kept their backs to the wind. The town was full of donkeys. At night they took shelter under a streetlight on the corner, because we had a power plant and everything, which made us feel as though we were riding on the crest of progress (consider the fact that that the first neon sign was given a blessing by the Bishop). We also had traffic lights, operated by a soldier with a light switch. In the calmer years, autumn was beautiful. At sunset, when the thrushes came to roost on the banana trees, my old man would go to work in the henhouse, always with the radio on in the background. From time to time the news would come echoing out from the Franklin in the kitchen. A reporter from Radio el Mundo was calling from the Sierra Maestra, an unforgettable name for all of us since they gave us *The Bandit of Sierra Madre*. Afterwards Glostora Tango Club would start, just as the chickens settled down to sleep.

At night we stuffed ourselves listening to Abelardo Pardales, the soap of the moment, radio-theatre full of hot-headed types that took place amongst slums and tangos, that was until a fire destroyed the power plant and La Punta was plunged into darkness for the rest of winter, cutting the series in half. Whilst the blackout lasted, there were more donkeys than ever. As you might imagine, they laid the blame with the Governor. Anecdotes about his obsession with barbecued meat, which it was said he preferred flame-grilled. They coined a gruesome story: the success reached him in Buenos Aires and he found out about it by telegram ('Power plant on fire') to which he responded immediately, 'Keep hot coals. I'll bring meat.'

That's what I was getting to. La Punta was the home of gossip. Two idiots crossing the street could unleash a cyclone. The most idiotic of all stretched out their hands saying 'two powers salute one another,' to get you talking. I guess that must have been how that one about Flamingo, our local roulette, got started, which filled us with pride because it was about Frank Sinatra. We'd fall for whatever we could get at that altitude. Another story we were sold was the one about the black guy from Los Plateros who came to town one day. He was an absolute sight who'd been kicked out of the group, and who would end up livening up the Saturdays at Tropicana. He wasn't even a proper black man. For us, who dreamed of the Harlem Globetrotters, he was more like a mulatto, and out of tune to boot. He was a far cry from the heights of Andy Moss, who could blow your mind and leave you floored when he launched into *Only You*. In any case, it would take us a long time to admit the con, and accept that he was a poor Brazilian from Porto Alegre. It's not hard to see it. How could you give up your music on a Saturday night while you float across the Tropicana dance floor with some chick? The music was the least of it. You could have danced to an ambulance siren; the aim wasn't to dance but to grip the unfortunate thing until you shatter her into this immaterial dust that leaves you speechless and dizzy, with your testicles like granite and on the edge of insanity.

Failing the Globetrotters we had to make do with the black ladies at Tropicana. I mean Tropicana II, the one in Havana, which sent the Mulatas de Fuego on an incredible tour. They came to La Punta via Chile, and everything kicked off. The Opera House organised three shows for over-18s only. They left the hall behind a police cordon, almost stark naked under their jackets, in the first ever bikinis to appear here. Amidst so many tempting mulattas, there were at least two that sang with real feeling, Elena Burke and Celia Cruz, but not even that could stop a religious fanatic from jumping from the stalls and shouting at the top of his lungs that everybody should leave the hall. It wasn't easy to understand what happened next, as over the next few days you could only piece together the disjointed phrases that you hear in snatches when grown-ups talk about serious things and God's involved. Not even the people with the best seats could explain in detail what went on. Celia was singing *Cao, cao, maní picao* when the believer jumped onto the stage and started shrieking. The mulattas' feathers froze, and the show was cut there and then. After an endless silence, they pounced on the believer. The curtain started to draw and the lights were being lowered; from then on, it's all a mystery. The street was buzzing with rumours about the extraordinary experience that the believer suffered at the hands of the mulattas, whose shadows were projected onto the screen as they hurled themselves onto the body stretched out on stage, as the last few reflectors were turned off. It was already becoming obvious to us that the mulattas had screwed him, one by one.

After the mulattas had gone, everything went back to normal. Tropicana took up its danceable routine again. The Opera House recovered from the Cuban-fest and that same Sunday we were watching a film. There was another cinema opposite but we never used to set foot in that one, since something had come down from above and killed a spectator, supposedly a black widow. Apart from being dangerous, the other cinema was a wasteland too that showed nothing but European films. The Opera House, on the other hand, was real life. I'm not going to start waxing lyrical about those dives, as people tend to do these days, which only serve for people to howl like animals from the moment the doors open until the matinee ends. I'm just saying that it was brimming with action. If you took a break it was to spit from the circle to the stalls or to have a wee at the back and run round to see it trickle under the front row. There was a moment of certain raptness, of the respect that should reign in a cinema: when Cantinflas, exclusive sweet seller from the famed Isnoa brand, appeared in the aisles shouting, 'Issnooo' chews, Issnooo' bonbons, Isssnooo' chocolate bars…,' he met with the scornful hiss of the audience ('So what the hell issss it then!?'). After which, he went back to palming off his merchandise quietly, and we returned to whatever we were doing, with no shortage of fleeting glances at the screen provided that whoever was in the film didn't start singing out of the blue, which always made everyone go crazy. Well, in one matinee like that we discovered the bearded guys, during the course of a news bulletin that also showed Bill Haley, a fact that I still remember today because everyone in the whole theatre started to jump up and down on their seats. Something told me that the bearded guys on the news were the guerrillas from Radio El Mundo that so fascinated my dad, whose adventures he would be engrossed in listening to while he cured a chicken or disinfected the troughs with methyline blue.

Aside from being a poultry farmer, my dad was also a banker and a qualified philosopher, thanks to Juanjo Arévalo. He never practised philosophy for fear of being affiliated with the Party, so he chose to work in the bank and set up the henhouses, and then had cards printed up that said 'Professor of Philosophy' and underneath, in tiny letters, 'chickens and eggs for sale'.

Meanwhile I whiled away the hours in the background, dedicated to such fascinating activities as lying belly up on the grain sacks or burying my arm down to my shoulder in chick feed. I felt something once; two Ballester Molinas, black and shiny. I never told a soul, nor did I take them out of the bag. I had a vague idea of what was going on. Now I had real motives for sticking around – I would pass the time by dipping my hands in to get to touch guns. My dad called me once on the telephone and asked me to go to the shed and bring back a package on my bike. He didn't have to tell me twice, which seemed to confuse him as he expected to have to repeat things until he went hoarse.

My house was a hide-out for dissidents and in some ways a haven too, because my aunt was married to a staunch Peronist. The police did used to come by, as the raids were carried out in Buenos Aires, cursing the mission that had fallen to them by chance. It was the actual Chief of Police that led the investigation. They would come in through the back door and never once mentioned the word raid. The only thing they were missing was a box of chocolates. They opened boxes with such care and without even looking inside, so that it seemed less like an inspection and more like nesting hedgehogs. They would have a cup of coffee in the living room with their berets on their laps under the watchful eye of my aunt, who was young and beautiful and loved her brothers and would have seen off a copper for the least display of rudeness. You could fuck with Perón, but not with my aunt. Then finally they would take somebody with them, either my father or my uncle, apologising again and again and promising to bring them back just as soon as everything died down, and indeed, they were always as good as their word.

Grandma, it's a bloody small world. Do you know where I heard about Juanjo? In Buenos Aires, through the paratroopers at the Primavera Guesthouse, that were selling San Sebastián chickens ('San Sebastián is more... chicken,' you know what I mean?). I never quite worked out how they ended up there. Juanjo was being accused of leading the Mayans to communism. That's why they had to invade Guatemala and follow it up with the resort attack, but something went wrong and so they fled in the little boat and floated around the Caribbean before turning to cannibalism.

Do you remember Bismarck González? He was my roommate in the Primavera, Venezuelan or something like that, perpetual medical student. Anyway, he was always coming up with plot ideas for me and it was him that led me to the paratroopers. That afternoon he had told me, 'I've got a *comiquita* for you,' which means comic strip in Venezuelan. 'I've got the title and everything: Garrapatenango.' But apart from his love for the genre, the Venezuelan was a nightmare roommate. He slept with a little bucket to hand, and every now and then he would wake up and dispense with about half a litre. When the bucket was full he would go over to the balcony, open one of the shutters and empty it out all over the patio, which made a real racket when it hit the third floor, amidst the sound of swearing from around the block. One night I woke up in the middle of the operation. When Bismarck was on his way back to bed I got a nasty feeling. Something wasn't right. The bucketful had sounded different. Bismarck couldn't have forgotten the bit with the shutters, surely? The stench started to permeate the room and I jumped out of bed, terrified, and switched on the light. It was worse than I could have imagined. Bismarck had gone the wrong way. The wardrobe was wide open and all the clothes were dripping wet. I couldn't bear to look at my blazer. Bismarck carried on sleeping soundly.

I met the first paratrooper at the Ferro ground, where Bismarck played baseball. His name was Ramón Masvidal, a blond guy with greenish eyes, and he told us the story of his landing at the resort between strikes. How had he come to this? The Revolution had grabbed him while he was studying at military school. One day a visit was announced, so the cadets stood up and in walked Che, right in the middle of the lesson. He went on to lecture to them for the next hour of maths. Ramón remembered noticing that Che's flies were undone. Then Ramón deserted for Florida and ended up being recruited in Miami. He was sent to the Antilles to a camp called Garrapatenango, an absolutely perfect title for a *comiquita*, which actually ended up being called *The Sacred Bird of Guatemala*.

I could already see it now on the front of *D'Artagnan*. It was my biggest ambition in life, although I also dreamt of something with the stature of *Misterix*. My work was only appreciated by the dimwits at the Primavera, whose names would occasionally turn up in the plots of my cartoons. So, Sapo Brentano might become a Formula One driver (Mike Brentano) or a Roman Legionnaire (Manlio Brentanus), something that was guaranteed to secure me a few *empanadas* in the downstairs canteen.

D'Artagnan took it as a joke. A banana fleet? Where did I get that from? Right, so the guys who sunk it were also from LAN Chile?[10] (that will have to be explained more clearly). 'Cilento, is this a historical cartoon?' the editor said, cornering me. (Cilento was my alias in *D'Artagnan*.) 'It's about war,' I clarified, to which he suggested that I should give it a certain D-Day quality, before throwing it onto his desk. 'I'll call you Monday,' he said, and we never saw one another again.

I didn't even hear back from *Silver Bullet*. I went from one magazine to the next and on the way met Vicky Walsh, a science columnist with a beautiful smile. She was a journalist's daughter. We stopped for a coffee at a café on the corner, and to break the silence I talked about the paratroopers. She didn't seem impressed, but she had heard of the camp; her dad was Rodolfo

Walsh and he'd been in Guatemala. In fact, it was him that had deciphered the secret codes about the invasion of the resort. Suddenly we spotted Borges waiting to cross the road and we guided him through the cars. The old man didn't stop criticising Cortázar for a second, which he carried on doing all the way to the library, where we finally left him safely. It was a miracle that we made it. Everybody wanted to help Borges to cross the road, so you always had someone trying to take him off you. Vicky was radiant. Seeing this photo from a distance, with her cracking up with laughter, it's hard to believe that she's the same girl that would end up surrounded by the army, firing a machine gun from the balcony only to turn the gun on herself.

Her father was the author of a book that my dad used to read voraciously in bed, the story of a massacre perpetrated by the trigger-happy crew. I remember him reading it as if he were witnessing a revelation. There wasn't any space left in my dad's heart. He hated the generals more than his classic enemies. In time I began to tie up a few loose ends; the massacre coincided with the period when I found the guns. My dad wouldn't hurt a fly, but he was a member of the rebels. As he got ill soon after that, we never got to talk about it, and I was left in charge of everything. It was a horrible time. Close to midnight, while I was smoking calmly in bed, I suddenly remembered the chickens and went out in my pants cursing. The snakes were clustered together close to the fence, their eyes shining with hunger. They could lurk there until sunrise, having not had a bite to eat all day. I lifted the feed buckets over the hedge, wracked with guilt, and carried on going. I didn't even look after the chicks any more. It was horrible, putting your hand into the coop to fish out the flattened carcasses. Of all the perverse creatures, the chicks were the worst. If one had a tiny crumb of food near its eye, another one would come and peck it until it drew blood, then the rest would all attack it and destroy it. Those were the sort of monsters we had back there. I saw it happen one morning when I removed the lid of the coop. It was when my dad died, when the henhouses went to ruin. I wasn't yet fourteen and I had to go through this.

Nothing, grandma. I came to say hello, that's all. I'm staying at the Hotel Dos Venados. I'm looking for a few clues – I want to get this cartoon off the ground again. I saw Mario yesterday. He gave me Juanjo's papers, including the box the bird was in. The quetzal's been had by maggots, he said. Then he gave me a hug and left. He is a gentleman, that guy. My dad kicked him out for being a Peronist, but Mario never even mentioned it. As we said goodbye he asked after Mimí Trujillo. Her name keeps coming up lately. Why should I see her? Because she was married to Rhadamés, he explained, the son of the butcher from the Antilles, a playboy who has bedded the most beautiful women in the world. Grandma: Do you know how far it is from Guatemala to the Dominican Republic? Me neither, to be fair, but I reckon they're pretty close, give or take a few beaches lined with coconut palms and ancient Mayan cities. All I can say is that Mimí was born around there, in a goat pen. Her name is Julia Celmira Marín. She ended up getting to Europe somehow and marrying a Trujillo who had an apartment in Paris and bred polo horses.

I called her yesterday. She has a charming voice, half-Punta, half-Caribbean. She thinks that her father-in-law wasn't quite as criminal as they say, but the political side of her family has remained remote. Mimí lives an austere life; by contrast, her ex-husband, if the internet is anything to go by, was executed by his associates from the Medellín cartel. Ramfis, the other brother, who was already colonel of the army at the age of six, killed himself on a French road with one of his lovers. Ramfis and Rhadamés, the boys were called, whose mum was evidently mad about opera. Ramfis' wife, who worked on crap movies, was Argentine as well. And as for Angelita, Mimí's sister-in-law, the Trujillo's little sister, she ended up dishing out petrol in a Florida gas station, although others say she entered a convent. There's a reason I mention her. You remember the paratroopers? The ones who ended up eating each other? Well, it was her yacht that got shipwrecked on the high seas.

I'm off now, grandma. If you'd at least open your mouth just once. You used to be a story-telling machine. Will you make any sense of anything I've been saying to you? Where will you go now? Shall I leave the radio on for you? *Cumbia villera*, grandma, the new national music. It's global warming. It's raining like the tropics! To think, they used to fine you for throwing water out onto the pavement. I'll come by again tomorrow. Would you like to go for a walk? Maybe I'll take you in your chair to my beach with the sand as white as sugar where the *comiquita* begins, on the very night that the *Chiquita Banana* lands on the coast, for the Worldwide Salsa Convention.

Notes

1. The 'GNC' in Spanish could be interpreted either as the Gran Novela Cordobesa or the Gran Natural Compromido, Argentina's state gas company.
2. 'Racauchi' was an Argentine soft drinks company from the Perón era, when foreign imports were largely banned.
3. Carqueja (*Baccharis trimera*) is a shrub-like plant with yellowish flowers found throughout the Amazon rainforest, as well as in tropical parts of Argentina, Paraguay and Uruguay. It is used in popular medicine to treat liver disease, rheumatism and diabetes.
4. Portuguese: 'children don't masturbate any more.'
5. A Latin American herb, also known as Larrea.
6. A Buenos Aires arts centre.
7. A tree native to Polynesia.
8. Feudal lords.
9. Buenos Aires' first fort, built in 1580 and now home to the administrative and government seats.
10. 'LAN Chile' stands for Línea Aérea Nacional, the largest Latin American airline, which operates out of Santiago, Chile.

Endnote

In terms of reality and fiction, there is a bit of everything in these pages, but all the characters and situations described in the story 'With the Whole World Crumbling, We Pick this Time to Fall in Love' belong to the sphere of the imagination and any similarity to real people or occurrences is pure coincidence. The same is true of 'It Wasn't Pacheco', 'Soul Radio' and 'Only Love Can Save You'. In any case, I must thank Milagros Belgrano Rawson, Jorge Nadal, Tanti Scarpati, Hugo Gramajo, César Pérez Laborda and José Pablo Feinmann for their contributions.

In 'Way of a Gaucho' and 'Them', on the other hand, fiction strays closer to reality. 'Garrapatenango' is the story of a novel: the roads travelled to tell the story of a landing in the Caribbean that had, in a way, started to gestate on the way home. This story appears in *Rosa de Miami* (Seix Barral, 2005) as an introduction with biographical touches.

Biographical note

Eduardo Belgrano Rawson was born in a small village in Argentina in 1943. In 1961, he moved to Buenos Aires where he studied Journalism and Cinema Studies and wrote film scripts. However, he gave up his profession as a journalist to dedicate himself exclusively to writing. His first novel, *No se turbe vuestro corazón* (*May your Heart not be disturbed*), published in 1974, dealt with the innocence of childhood and the merci-lessness of war. Five years later, his book *El náufrago de las estrellas* (*Shipwreck of the Stars*) was awarded the Premio del Club de los Trece, and confirmed Eduardo Belgrano Rawson as one of Argentina's most brilliant narrators. Five more novels followed, including, in 2006 *El Mundo se derrumba y nosotros nos enamoramos* (published here as *Washing Dishes in Hotel Paradise*).

Belgrano Rawson is also one of the jurors for the prestigious prize Premio Clarín in Buenos Aires. Translated into many dif-ferent languages, Belgrano Rawson's writing has been com-pared to that of literary figures such as Ernest Hemingway and Michael Ondaatje.